BLUE EYES

Body Parts

FREDERICK H. GILBERT

For book orders, email orders@traffordpublishing.com.sg

Most Trafford Singapore titles are also available at major online book retailers.

Please be advised:

828 words of the 35000 word text of book, less than 1% contain sexual context or references. This author consider the sexual acts contents essential to the book and the understanding to real life sexual situations experienced by the disabled.

Printed in Singapore.

ISBN: 978-1-4907-0421-0 (sc)
ISBN: 978-1-4907-0422-7 (hc)
ISBN: 978-1-4907-0423-4 (e)

Trafford rev. 02/22/2014

 www.traffordpublishing.com.sg

Singapore
toll-free: 800 101 2656 (Singapore)
Fax: 800 101 2656 (Singapore)

Dedication

To all my fictional characters, whom I will
never forget in my fictional memory!

CONTENTS

CHAPTER 1

Another Beginning

Doctor Peterson

I have flown many of flights from San Diego, during my life span thus far, e.g. Canada, Mexico Philippines, Thailand and to many cities, towns and villages of the United States. Now I was flying all the way to Russia, to a job as a Public Relations Consultant at Russian Hospital at a city that I cannot even pronounce.

Doctor Robert Peterson asked me to take this assignment because he thought that I would have a more open mind to how the Russians deal with their disabled population.

Doctor Peterson and I served on the same committee was on the Bi-national Emergency Medical Care Committee of the California-Baja and California Council.

Peterson wrote me, saying the Russians were interested in changing their public relations method of how they portrait the disabled population and more important their image. They wanted someone to design an appeal campaign on how to raise funding methods from solicitations and donation of contributors from the Western and European markets. He said the delegations from The Ministry of Labor And Social Development were visiting a rehabilitation center in San Diego.

Meeting Russian Delegation

I was not really looking for a job at the time, when the Russians when they approached me at the rehabilitation center with Doctor Peterson leading them to me.

After a long discussion with them, I just did not see what they are trying to do with me except use me as a PR poster boy since there were many Public Relation firms to choose from.

I know very little of the Public Relation field except for few classes I took as electives under Professor Center at San Diego State University. I not sure of what exactly I was really going to do there but the Russian made very finically appealing, the salary, the flight, my personal attendant or Care Give; Private Residential Suite with service staff and a new experience.

At the end, I do not really care about leaving San Diego, I just want something to do different. I am very bored and just tired of retirement.

Therefore in this trip, I now was wondering what this new trip, new assignment and my new adventures were going to be like.

I do not feel confident that I can solve their problems but I believe what they really want a handicapped to parade around as some type of role model, just another fund raising poster child for their new funding and contributing methods in their new foundered democracy.

My thoughts to myself, as I preparing for my trip was, "The Russians are spending a lots of money on me. I better, come up with something while I am there".

Resume

I have over forty years, I been a founder, director of, or consultant and retired volunteer to many agencies in United States, Canada, Thailand the Philippines as well as Mexico.

As for some of agencies I founded, directed or department head they were: Sharp Rehabilitation Center as the Recreation Therapy and Volunteer Coordinator; The Physically Handicapped Olympic Games; Recreational Services for the Handicapped; Camp Friendship's Day and Residential Camps. During these responsibilities, I had to do a lot of fund raising events to carry on many of these programs.

I am quite an old hand of being use for public relations and I have also used my handicap image to get what I wanted to help built the programs I envisioned in helping the disabled but it was really for own my ego.

CHAPTER 2

Another Leaving

Goodbyes

My entire luggage was pickup early at my hotel suite where I spent the two days saying goodbye to my family and to my friends, Carmen, Michael, Ivonne, Janely, and course Jose, my Mexican jester, RC and his wife.

Mary Lou and Jereme said their goodbye at the nudist camp where was living, De Anza Spring Resort, at a farewell party the camp gave me the night before coming to the hotel.

Mary Lou and Jereme were friends for over twenty-five years. They would be the only friends, outside the nudist camp, who come to the camp to see me. They would not take their clothes off, but walked around the camp un-impressed with the nudity around them (Maybe not so much for Jememe, young man.)

Rosa

I had a prostitute, Rosa, stayed with me the two nights at the hotel, while I was visiting. She helped me get dressed each morning before she left for the day.

Rosa was my friend and favorite prostitute who was a beautiful young light black lady, who on some days did not charge me, but did so only when she needed it. She usually charged me between, $50 and $100 a night, depending what I wanted that night or afford.

Since I was leaving for Russia, she only let me pay her $50 for the two days, that because she had to take a cab back and forth as well as a baby sitter.

She has a good-looking six-year-old boy, but she has been fighting Child Protection Services from taking him away because of her illicit job as a prostitute, which paid her very well and a lot more than any other job she could of find.

We spent some time together with her son, who loves me telling him ghost stories.

She is a very smart lady and talented as a creative dancer. She tried to break in to the professional as a dance performer in the arts but just could not break in because she lack paid performance experiences.

Rosa did not trust men anymore, including me, as a suitor, we were just good friends. I am really going to miss her friendship and sex.

CHAPTER 3

The Airport

Unarmed

Entering the airport security checkpoint I carry just my Laptop and a "purse-wallet"; it that hangs around my shoulder. It is easier for people to take my money, credits, identification and my store my business cards. When traveling, I sometime carry a small bag of tools to repair my arms in an emergency and car control devices that I put on a rental car (an "L" shape bar that I attach to turn signal arm with my knee and a driving hook on the steering wheel), if I am renting one.

I am been asked to take out my personal belonging from my pockets onto a big tray. "But I don't have anything; I cannot put things in my pockets, so I cannot take them out." Seeing my situation, the security man passes me to another person who now waves a detector wand over my arms and my body. I said to them, "Don't worry, I am unarmed!" They laughed at my joke as they pass me thru the checkpoint with scanner still buzzing since my artificial arms was partially metal.

That's all I carry on board a airplane with me, beside my artificial arms and of course my laptop.

Laptop

My old laptop that Mary Lou, my friend, gave me several years ago. I take my laptop everywhere I go. I use my laptop every chance I get, like now!

If there is table around, I will pull out my laptop.

My trackball attached to the outer pocket of the computer case cover with Velcro closure, the USB plug already hooked up to the computer so that I place on the floor and use with my feet. Mostly I use a chopstick to type, which attached to the pencil holder mounted on the outside of my computer. But in public, I use my right hook to type. But more and more lately I use my hook to type because I am losing my teeth, so holding on to chop stick is getting harder to grasp.

CHAPTER 4

I Became Dinner

To Be My Last Flight Home

As I stared across the runway from the window of the waiting room, I can see the Jim Aires building where once stood the old Lindbergh Field Airport Terminal. It was from there that I was supposedly to have my last trip home to Stockton, California.

Bears

Many years ago, I lost my both my arms to a couple of bears in a circus accident; I was only 8 years old with a small boy body then, I was just a small meal for the bears and a big lost for me.

On September 18, 1952 to be more exact, at a ball park in Tecate, Baja California, Mexico on the border with the U.S. was just 45 miles from this airport.

Flying across My Memories

It was 12 days after I lost one and one half my arms.

I was waiting there for a DC3 to take me to LA airport to transfer to a DC7 flight to San Francisco to meet another DC3 to take me to Stockton, California our regular home during the school season.

At the Lindbergh Field Airport Terminal, I laid in a gurney; an ambulance had just brought me in from the old Tijuana General Hospital.

I had just crossed the border at San Ysidro, where an U.S. Customs agent search the ambulance and then started to take my bandages off to look if I carrying any counter bans, but seeing the blood, plus smelling the bad odor of gangrene he then let us pass.

As I remembered, my mom and me were waiting at the terminal, there was a large crowd around me and a few reporters, who happen to be covering another story at the airport, they came over asking my mother what happen to me.

A pilot of the DC3 that I was going on, notice the commotion, took pity on me and came over to me, gave me his wings and started talking to my mom. He seen the flight tickets my mom was holding and noticed that was his flight we were going on.

After learning that I had little time to live, he quickly dashed to the ticket counter; he grasped an old type stand microphone and made an announced that his plane was going to leave 15 minutes earlier. He then told those passengers already there, to line up and to board as faster as possible after I was loaded me between two set of seats that were facing each other on the gurney with my mother next to me.

I was watching the other late passengers scrambling to the plane once it was learned it was taking off earlier than scheduled.

When I arrived in LA, there were many reporters and men with big cameras, were there covering my transfer to the DC7 waiting at other end of the runway directly from the DC3, with it engines still running. As soon as we were seated on the plane, it took off toward San Francisco where many more reporters and cameramen where waiting to see me make another transfer to a waiting DC3 at the terminal gate, but I need to urinate badly and the restroom was too small for two people. No one thought to bring a urinal and no one seemed to want to give up a coffee cup.

Some man hearing of my urgent need lifted me from my gurney, rushed me into the terminal to the restroom. He stood me on my legs, pulled down my shorts to urinate, he quickly lifted my pants, hearing me crying from the pain of my amputations touching his arms when I finished. All the while reporters were watching taking notes and photographers taking flashed pictures of me in the restroom, then the man rushed back to the waiting DC3 that soon left the terminal while I was still being put back on the gurney. Thanks guy, whoever you are!

Hot Racing Nun Race

At Stockton Airport, there were only a reporter, no cameramen and no ambulance waiting.

It was a small airport then but my mother had previously call Sister Rosa Timothy, who was supposedly to have an ambulance there but could not get the hospital to provide one.

Therefore, they transfer me from the gurney to the back seat of her old Desoto.

Sister Rosa Timothy asked two motorcycle cops, who happen to be at the airport, if they would give us an escort with red lights and sirens. They looked into car, seen how badly I was and then said to the sister to follow them to San Joaquin Hospital.

I could see the cops were in front of us but the sister had soon passed them. I could hear them behind us until the sister outran a train at a railroad crossing leaving the officers on the other side of the tracks.

The Doc That Saved My Life

A doctor, who name I do not know, who was leaving hospital for vacation, seen the commotion at the parking lot, looking at my wounds he then orders that I be taken right away to the operating room.

He amputates the rest of my left half of my remaining arm, because gangrene had badly set in most of my upper body, I could see him cutting away my tissues and nerve endings, as yet the sedatives and anesthesia had not set in. *At that moment the pain was so great, even with all the medication they gave me, when I felt that I was not worth saving!*

I learned later from my mother, he place me on intravenous blood transfer with mixed in pure oxygen, a technique that he had just developed for treating gangrene.

I Accepted My Disability Then As A Plus

I came from a poor family but the accident brought a lot of attention and lot of gifts to my family, mostly me.

I accepted my disability then as a plus. My sisters, (five of them) became jealous of my higher status for receiving lots of stuff and toys, electrical typewriter from the Iris Club, a model from Rockwell, which I never thanked them for, and felt guilty all my life. I got to travel to UCLA Child Prosthetic Center at least every three to six months on a train.

On one trip I get to meet Grace Kelly, was an American film actress and wife of Prince Rainier III of Monaco.

I got to meet lot of movie stars, went to movies studios and amusement places.

Many consider me as having had courage and being brave for doing absolutely nothing except being a crippled.

For years my handicapped fed my ego, my "me" and my importance. For many years, I would have given up my legs for even more attention.

From the accident, I had all that attention and the physical touching that went with being a crippled poster child.

As I became a teenager and a young adult the poster child image started to fade. It faded all the way down to nothing as a disabled adult.

The need inside me, wanting to be a hero and having a courageous image stayed as my persona the rest of my life, but I still longed for all that public attention and the graving for physical touching that was getting when I was younger.

I Am What I Am

As an adult, I believed I became a sinister looking person to some people, not to be look at, even to talk to or be touched as they may get whatever afflictions they thought I had.

Many of folks would take a quick look at me as they tried not to be noticed.

A number of parents would avoid being in the same aisle at stores or waiting at same line I was, to avoid children from asking about what happen to my arms.

On one occasion, as one of my able-bodied camper introduced me, as "Capthooks" to her mother, who suddenly slapped her very hard and pulled her away as I tried to explain to the mother it, was my real nickname. I often wondered what the little camper thought about her mother or me afterward.

What's In the Name?

I now use the word "Unique" instead of "handicapped" and "disabled" used interchangeable, as I never like the phrase "Physically Challenge".

Before my favorite word was "crippled". At times, I am not disabled or handicapped, like when I drive my car or have sex. Crippled simply signify that my body has a defect, that all.

But in the United States it is a very politically not correct term and I have been damned by the political correct handicapped (disabled) for using it.

When in Thailand I wrote for the "Beautiful Unique Thai Fashion Show" "Concept Recommendations and Suggestions" report:

What is the new significance of using the word "Unique" instead of:
Disabled, Handicapped or Physically Challenged?
It is a new start!
We want to be seen, our chance to have a truer image of
our lives as Thais and foreigners alike in Thailand.
Being disabled is different for each of us in the major
classification of disabilities e.g. Para, blind, CPs, deaf,
hard of hearing, MR, mental ill, . . . and etc.
Then underneath each of these subcategories are even more
sublevels of different level of abilities or subtype of the same
disabilities therefore making for a very "unique", individual.
Use the name "Unique" as a class for all of us who are different
from each other, instead of general term of disability, "physically
handicapped, physically challenged, crippled or gimps".
Just as the word Thais represents many different
unique cultural groups in Thailand.
We are "Unique" individuals or persons; each
expressing our uniqueness in being different.
Uniqueness gives us our own individual identity! Not a classification

CHAPTER 5

From the Waiting Room Window

Boarding time

"Attention, all passengers for flight 207 to New York City will be boarding shortly. Will all passengers with special needs, parent with small children and unaccompanied minors, please start boarding at Gate 12 now?"

Now, I have to pack up my laptop now and continue my writing aboard the plane after I settle in with my laptop for the long flight to New York.

It hard for me to hold a book or magazine while in flight, so on my laptop I write or play games, like Spider or Coin Dumper to help pass the time during my flight.

Stewardess

I always wanted to sit by the window on my flights, but making it harder for the flight attendant to help me if there are other passengers between the steward and myself.

This is where I really get some good attention from beautiful stewardesses if lucky, that I if not a male steward.

Usually she will spend extra time with me to straps me into my seat and hands feeds me because they are serving sandwiches, of which I cannot handle well in flight. If it was a hot plate, I can feed myself after the flight attendant open all items on tray are opened for me and given a spoon instead of fork and a straw.

Sometimes after getting started on a flight, they move me to first class because there more room for them to care and strap me in.

Flying in Style

This time, I am flying First Class courtesy of the Russian. I know I will receive extra personal service.

I felt little embarrassed because I had to be very casual dressed and always had to wear short shorts while I traveled alone in order to take myself to urinate by pulling up my short with my hook. Usually black colored shorts so color helped hide urine stains from not being able to shake dry after urinating.

During a long flight a stewardess often sit with me to talk and pass the time away.

On one flight to New York, I talk to a stewardess out of committing suicide during her flight. We later had a date in New York, said she was getting help, but I never seen or spoke to her again.

Got, To Go Now!

"Second and last call"—**Got, To Go Now!**

Next Stop New York City

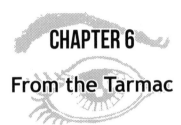

CHAPTER 6

From the Tarmac

Well first class is classy. I seem to be the only one in first class. It must be the high gas price; even the rich cannot afford first class.

The beautiful stewardess had just strapped in, I cannot wait to chat with her on this 5 hour flight.

Looking across the tarmac from this plane, which waiting to take after clearance, I could again see Jim Aires building much closer.

India Street

Just up from Jim Aires on Harbor Drive and above Highway 5 freeway is India Street, this is where I grew up in my preteen years.

My mother, work in the late 50 to mid sixty for Convair, a Division of General Dynamics that is located just north of Jim Aires.

My mother only had an eighth grade education but rose from shipping packer to shipping inspector while working there.

She also turns in an idea how to pack a Atlas missile with all of it parts into one load by submitting a coke glass bottle and placing it inside a milk carton, she receive $15,000 for her idea.

Having troubles with my arms, my mother talked to some metallurgist at her job site and told him about a problem I had with my artificial arms shoulders that kept breaking down. She took one of my arms to work to show him the problem. He designed a part and made it out of titanium, then a top-secret alloy.

However, there was a problem, "given it to me", because there was no ways to legally to have Convair give it to me.

So mom made it all the way to top management, where they decided to have a little press ceremony and toss it over the security fence to me.

However, then I was worried that a Russian spy would take my arms from me to get the secret metal. However, it never happened.

Flying Across My Hometown Memories

As the plane lifted passed Point Loma area, I could see Montalvo Street that run parallel to Nimitz Boulevard, where I lived with my forth wife, her daughter and my son.

OB

Further out, I could see Long Branch Avenue in Ocean Beach, "OB" as it known by, where I moved from San Francisco to start my retirement years.

The one thing I really remember about in OB was a beautiful homeless blond woman who was my attendant who would give me a blowjob every time she bathed me. Believe me, I figured out many reasons to take a bath.

Sharpe

Susan Sharpe, my psychologist, is right underneath the plane, just off Rosecrans in Point Loma.

I spent over 5 years in therapy with her trying to overcome the loosing of my son for the second time and when they moved to Wisconsin.

Tanna, my adopted daughter and Ricky from my fourth marriage, refused to talk or write to me. I could not understand why, or I refused to acknowledge why, we were very close before my wife and broke up.

October 5th

To the right is where mother is buried at the Rosecrans National Cemetery The whole family and moms old friends gather at Cabrillo National Monument near my mother grave site every October 5th, to mark her passing. This was the last time this we would ever meet again, we all were getting old and dying off.

This was the last time I would ever see my whole family and my mother's grave again. From Russia, I am planning to head back to Thailand to take advantage of their retirement Visa program, to live out the rest of my life there and where sex is much cheaper.

Baja

As plane made a right turn over the ocean, I could see Tijuana, Mexico to the left. I could remember working at Tijuana Hospital and the School for the Handicapped.

I also held OPPI Games in and out of the Jai Alai Hippodrome in downtown Tijuana.

I lost six hundred dollars of my own money on the Olympic game there. I was promise funding and support from the Governor of Baja California Both never paid.

La Jolla Camp Ground

Even if could not see it from my plane was, about 60 miles south of was Ensenada.

My son Freddie and I would camp there for the summer.

The owner, was a very close friend of my dad, whom I lost 66 years ago. He began crying when he learns that I was his friend son.

While camping there, Freddie, a teenager at the time, would switch my full can of beer for his empty can of beer without me knowing it.

Flying Over the Back Country

As the plane flew east over the mountains, I remembered Cuyamaca School Camp, where I was a camp counselor and Laguna Shiners Camp where I had Camp Friendship Residential Camp for handicapped children.

Tecate

In the distance on the south side of the border fence that marks the Mexican and the gringo sides of the border, I can see I could also see Tecate, Baja California, where I lost my arms from the plane. It is about 36 Miles / 59 Km miles southeast along the border and southwest of Jacumba, California.

My arms still buried on the Mexican side of the border. I guess I have a true 'hands across the border policy'.

One of my great-great grand fathers, Agustín Vicente C Zamorano (1798-1842), provisional Governor of Alta California, when it was Spanish territory. I knew the date, because I have book *on my computer* by *George L. Harding, (1934). Don Agustín V. Zamorano: Statesman, Soldier, Craftsman, and California's 1st Printer.*

I wished *Zamorano,* could have just saved me one square inch of Santa Barbara, I could have been rich.

On my father side, we consider ourselves Californianos, not Mexicans, so say my aunt Eva.

Nudist Camp

Then the nudist camp came into view, we were flying just a little north of it. De Anza Spring Resort is where I lived nearly four years. I had just sold my fifth Wheeler and the "improvements" site and vacated before I left to the hotel airport.

Many of times, I sat outside on my patio, which I designed and built, watching airlines using the same route that I am now.

I would not need to get dressed to go swimming, hiking, and using the gym, or to our little store (Bear Country Store) or to go to our Saturday nights at the Bare Club Bar with our own full stocked liquor bar.

I tried to say it was for practical reasons that I lived there, however, I was interested in seeing young naked women and I had high hope of lots of sex, sex part never happened, as I wanted.

What sex I got, was on two different occasions who husbands wanted me to fuck their wives be in front of them as a 'turn on' for them. Sadly, however, it only happens twice with two different couples.

Nevertheless, I did get to enjoy the nudist life style and eventually made it my own life style.

I started to write this book there.

Rina

I was not going to tell anyone of the most painful experience that happen to me at the nudist camp. Mostly as reverence to her family, however I think she would have wanted to include her in my writings.

There were some women who I had phone sex with whom I really wanted real sex with but had always put me off. Rina was one of them.

Rina was a girl from my college, who used me as a personal counselor for long time and subsequently started having phone sex with her.

I was very sexual infatuated with her and became very platonically in love with.

I would masturbate as best as I could by rubbing my penis on the bed or sofa as we imagined have sex with each other. I would pretend I was having sex with her, as she would describe touching and masturbate herself or with her use of a vibrator, she had just bought.

She lived with her parent and they were strong Jehovah Witnesses, but inside her bedroom, she had a secret life of her own.

For over five or six years she had a sexual affair with a married professor from her college. Rina added a person from the internet to her lover affair, sending him over $3000 as a loan to help him buy a car, which he never paid back.

Little by little, I encouraged her to put a time limit on her affairs, to get them to marry her or quit wasting her time with them and her to get on with her life. None of them really wanted to change the status quote with her and wound up with me as her only true friend, she would tell me so.

Rina was always telling me of her sexual affair or phone sex experience with these men. It was not hard for our conversations on the phone to turn to phone sex. The more we had phone sex the more I wanted to be there with her having sex.

Every time we would setup a date, Rina would windup canceling. I did love her very platonically, but broke off with her after she cancels a long planned date; because she made me feel I was not equal to the other men she wanted.

I did not see or talk to her in years.

Rina became a character, the Princess, in my book, "Humpty Dumpty".

One day I get a call from her, Rina was apologetic for the way she had treated me.

Rina told me she had broken off with her husband five month prior because she had terminal cancer and had become very depressed.

Rina had stopped the chemotherapy and stopped all her medications. Said she was feeling much better but the doctor told without therapy and medications she would die.

Rina wanted to talk to me, however because since I broke off the relationship as it was, she could not get herself to call me.

I could hear in her voice that she really did want to talk with me. Therefore, I relented and told her I would come to see her, if she wanted me to.

Rina said yes. I asked her where she was. She said, "Right here!"

That puzzled me. I question I her, "Where?"

"I am across the ravine, here at the De Anza Spring Motel. I, been here for a few days watching you, making sure that I would not be disturbing any of your love affairs." She said kidding.

I looked across, I saw her there standing naked at her motel door. Without saying anything, I rush out on my fifth wheeler towards her hotel, down and up through the sanding ravine.

Rina met me at the top; we hugged and kissed each other. She invited me inside her room.

Her head was still bald from the chemotherapy and had a large square bandage on her left side of head. Rina told me that it held a shunt to drain accumulating fluids from the cancer site. When the pain became too great for her, she would go to her doctor to have it drained. Not understanding why, I was not, put off by it, I have seen many shunts in my work.

As if as nothing had happen between us, we were embracing each other with one of my legs wrapped between hers holding her tight against my body, as I had no arms to hold her. She had her arms around my neck as I pulled her up tightly against my chest.

Rina started to cry, so I put her down. She again was apologetic.

I said trying to lighten the experience. "That the past was a done deal," I told her.

Rina said she had a lot of mixed feeling about coming. "I didn't want to hurt you again but because of my cancer, I just did not want to be alone. I just do not want to be in a hospice care facility or with my parents, but just wanted to be with you.

"The only one I feel I can talk to is you. I wanted someone to with me when I die. You have always been straight with me. I do not want to die without talking with you." She finished emotionally as if she was asking too much of me.

"I'm here, I here for you, I still care for you very much." It was, the only thing, I could say to her.

Tears again ran down her cheeks, as I sip them off with my lips.

We spent the night together. In the morning, Rina got dressed and came with me to my fifth wheeler to dress me so we could go out to get a pizza and soft drinks at the nearby Chevron gas station on Highway 8.

We did not have much sex, we talked mostly with her touching, playing with my penis until I finally climaxed, and I gave her oral sex.

We spent most of next few days at her motel room with occasional outings to the nearby attractions.

Then Rina helps me clean-up my bachelor type living style and move her in with me. She did not have much with her but she still had her vibrator with her.

The vibrator was the source of a lot humor that followed the next few months. After a while, our lives became routine without any reference to her cancer.

As time went on, we started having lots of sex and watched x-rated films I had. Each night as we fell asleep, she would be holding my penis in her hand, as it was my hands, I did not have.

One night I felt her hand tighten around my penis hard, waking me. Surprised, I looked into her eyes, she smiled, her eyed closed, stopped breathing and she died. There was nothing I could do for her, we talked several time what I could do when her time came! Rina said, "Just let me die with you beside me." I laid beside her for awhile, weeping with my tears falling on her face, wanting to make sure I was there for her as her body cooled.

I called the 911 operator to notify authority, but I knew I could not do more, I sat the rest of the evening outside watching the stars, knowing in the back of my head, this was the way she wanted to happen for her, when her day would come.

We were a good distance from the nearest paramedic unit, The San Diego County Sheriff arrived within a half an hour, while paramedic unit took an hour or so for them arrive from El Cajon. They pronounce her dead at the scene. They arranged to have the coroner to pick up her body.

The paramedics and the local Sheriff had left, since it was going to be a couple of hours until the coroner picked up her body.

I remind outside sitting under the stars, it was sometime between that time, I sat there cursing at the whole world and to any gods in the universe above, "Why did it all have to end it?"

I called her parents, but as soon as they heard my voice, they knew what I was about to say. They had expected the call would come from me.

Earlier in the month while visiting her parents in Escondido, Rina went to see her lawyer. Rina gave him instruction of what to do was her body, left her car to me and gave most of insurance money to me. Rina said wanted to pay for my badly needed dental work.

CHAPTER 7

The Armless Clown

Full of Shit

I wanted to stay in New York City for a couple of days to reminisce when I once lived in New York City but I had no attendant with me to dress me, so I was scheduled to leave that same night for Russia.

Lucky for me, I been having bowel movement problems, where I do not have one for over a week or more at time I think they call it "FOS", Full of Shit! That meant I could not have a bowel movement until I got to my room at the new hospital residence, then forcing myself to take 60 mg of Milk of Magnesia on a regular bases after arriving.

However, now I got plenty of time to reminisce and to write about my stay in New York City as I fly over the Atlantic.

Armless Clown

It is strange, that a number of years before coming to Welfare Island, I started to write a book, "The Armless Clown", about an armless rag doll clown who is thrown into a pile of broken toys at a Goodwill Industries toy recycle center. Like the movie, "Toys Story", the place, becomes animate after the center closed for the night.

In my story, the armless clown, help accomplish the uniting of the broken toys with the good unbroken toys that surrounded the toy repair table.

The clown had helped connect both communities (Welfare Island & New York City) with carts that acted as if they were ferryboats.

22

The armless clown had fallen in love with the good toy's mayor daughter. The Mayor did not think it was good for his political career that his daughter was having an affair and was seen making love together. He also did like the idea that she would become a slave to the clown, in helping him in daily activities. Therefore, the mayor told the armless clown to, 'just disappear', or he would stop the cart ferries and band the broken toys from participating in any more with the good toys community.

I actually felt like I lived out the story of the, "The Armless Clown", on Welfare Island.

Welfare Island

In the East River under the Queensboro Bridge, opposite the U.N. Building lies Welfare Island, as it was call. It once held three or four different hospitals but when I worked in late sixty there only two, Collier and Goldwater were left operating at the time. The third abandoned hospital stood at Goldwater end of Welfare Island was abandon for some reason with hospital equipment and hospital beds decaying for some time. It was this abandoned hospital that was used in the closing scenes in the movie, "The French Connect".

Nurse "Gretchen"

While I was living at nurse's dorm on Welfare Island, I thought was a dream come true, that in the same building where I lived, there were be 250 nurses waiting to have sex with me.

Wrong! There were very strict rules that I and the other males who lived on the one segregated floor of the nurse's resident had to follow. If caught on any other floor, except the basement floor (Laundry Room), we would have been thrown out immediately and as well as any nurses who were with us or in the nurses rooms.

There seem to be a retired nurse on each floor who acted like a dorm proctor. They never seem to sleep, checking the halls and every elevator doors when they opened. I would often ride with the young beautiful nurses to the nurses floors to say my goodbyes, hoping to get a date, but there waiting at every floor was Nurse "Gretchen" waiting at the elevator doors to make sure I did not get off on to their floor.

Killing Them Dead

Goldwater was where I work; however, New York University paid my salary.

I cannot remember how many floors it was, but the Recreation Department, had many diversified staff members with each having a different recreational and activity skills. They would serve one ward in afternoon and another one in the evening until each had completed all the wards by the week's end. Staffing was straggled so there were staffs to cover the weekend too.

There was a piano player who entertain in a nightclub fashion and beautiful woman who could speak seven different languages fluently, their names I cannot remember.

I had a mixed role from recreational activities, storytelling, entertainment, special occasion's celebration and just making an ass of myself, which the patients really seemed to enjoy.

"I was killing them dead!" literary, some my patients actually died laughing at my jokes or antics, the doctors told me that I had to tone my programs down so they would not run out of patients to care for.

Mildred

Because I was young, crazy and disabled, many of the patients and I became very close.

There was Mildred, an old black woman, who actually died while I was joke around in ward.

She was like a grandmother to me, were shared our pasts with each other and old movies.

When I worked at night, I often when to her after work and said goodnight to her until she died.

She would tell often how much the patients and she appreciated me coming to the ward and making them forgot they were in the hospital.

The Walking Priest

Then there was "The walking priest" who could not walk no more. I think he was the model used in the movie "Forest Gump", when he walked back and forth across the United States.

He and I talked a lot about religion, not about the bible but the humanity of Jesus and the lost of the true meaning of Christianity. "The people come first not the church!" He once told me.

I was unhappy with his care there and wondering why the church was not caring for him. I made a visit to the New York Diocese; talk to a number of persons with my concerns and finally got an audience with the Archbishop.

Later that week, Church officials came to the hospital in a black limousines and a private ambulance. They talked to him for hours convincing him to go to one of the catholic hospital in the area.

I knew, that he knew, he was dying and I could see he was suffering a lot. I hoped that he would be receiving better care there.

Juanita

One young man, who volunteered for me, fell in love with a beautiful young Cuban girl patient named Juanita, who was born with no sexual organs, no vagina nor an urination opening, who at birth had to have a tube place from her kidneys into a leg bag that she hated to wear. She would hide it by wearing long dresses and empting the bag often. She also sprayed the areas with a de-odor chemical, hoping to conceal the urine smell that came from the bag.

They became very involved, he wanted to marry her but she held off because she was unable to tell him of her situation.

One evening during my rounds, I caught her on the ward balcony crying. I asked her what was wrong, she replied by telling me her personal sex situation with her boyfriend.

I told her there were alternate ways of satisfying him other than sexual intercourse. I suggest that I talked with her social worker and setup a patient conference with her boyfriend and her.

At the conference, she revealed everything. At first, he was confused about her situation. As she spoke, she made it sound like that her lack of sex organs was the reason not to marry him.

He was adamant, that he was truly in love with her.

After we got both them to have a frank discussion about sex and alternative methods of sexual gratifications, they left with some ideas to try out in their relationship.

The last I heard of them was they were married and did or were planning to adopt children with her type of disabilities.

Chuck

Then there was Chuck, a severely disabled adult cerebral palsy who communicated with a talk board. Letters and phrases arranged on a lapboard, attached to his wheelchair, for Chuck to point to and communicate.

He moved around in his wheelchair, pushing it backward with one leg.

He was goofy looking man in his late thirty's or early forty's, but very smart and made himself known, specially to the young nurses in the NYU internship program.

One of the young nurses in the program befriended Chuck. She spent a lot of her free time together, kidding around with him.

She would tell everyone that Chuck was her boyfriend and he inturn he would claim she was his girlfriend. He had her name written on his talk board, followed by the word "girlfriend".

On one of my night off, I was walking around the island at night, when I notice a wheelchair floating upside down in the boat ramp area. Upon getting closer, I could see it was Chuck wheelchair. I could see him far out, almost to the East River current, bobbing in the water.

I yelled out to a nearby security guard building for help.

One guard and I waited out into the ice-cold water to get to Chuck, who trying to drown himself. He was too bottom-heavy as he was not able to get his head into the water, but you could hear him crying and angrily trashing about.

We pulled him ashore as more help came and a police car came with blankets covered Chuck who by now was in hyperthermia from the cold water.

After bring him back from the emergency room at the hospital to his room I asked Chuck what was going on.

After struggling to sit up, I cranked him up into a seating position with my foot and motion for his talk board with my head. He explains on his talk board, with tears running from his face, that the nurse, who befriends him, had told him she was getting married.

Chuck intern nurse girlfriend had rushed to the emergency room as news traveled through the nurse's grapevine.

I broke the news of happen to Chuck and why. Then upon asking the nurse trainee, why she did called him her boyfriend?

She replied in tears "Just to make him feel good, I didn't think he really believed it, I was just kidding around with him!"

I said to her, "We have hearts, too!" She then ran to see Chuck.

Chuck became my inspiration to write my book "Humpty Dumpty".

The Would-Be Ballerina

The would-be ballerina who seemed to have been born backward, her head, and arms were facing opposite her torso and her paralyzed legs faced up, she was confine, head down, to a gurney with big wheelchair type wheels. She could maneuver her gurney fair well.

I often lay down on the floor to carry out long conversation and have eye contact her, she like that, because she would not need to hold her head up, straining her neck. There was a hole on the gurney beneath her face, so she could see, eat and talk through; she also had a mirror attach below the gurney to help navigate the floor of the hospital's wide halls and elevators. Sometime she used it to talk to people, but she had to adjust mirror every time, from navigation mode to seeing people mode.

Her interest was the ballet, she seemed to know everything there was to know about the ballet and she drew beautiful picture of ballet costumes and sets. She would pull herself over the front of her gurney when she drew or wanted to use her hands freely from the gurney. She had to brace the end of her gurney as not to fall over when a good part of her body was over the gurney front edge. She had around her bedsides two-night stands full of magazines, books and tapes on the subject of ballet

Yet she never been to a ballet or met a ballerina in her lifetime.

While I was in New York City, just walking around the theater area trying to find affordable live theater tickets, I saw the office to the New York Ballet Company and went in. I asked to see the director, who did listen to my story. He directed me to a ballet theater to talk to a Ballet Madam.

The Madam seemed to be in charge of everything, nevertheless, she quietly listen to my request if I could bring my would-be ballerina to a dress rehearsal.

Madam agreed, so I set up an ambulance, an orderly, a nurse and a young intern to accompany her to the theater, as the Hospital Director requested as a condition to take her out of the hospital for field trip.

I waited for her at the theater preparing for her seating by propping her up backward of her normal position in a regular ambulance type gurney with the wheels in the clasped mode. I also already cued in the performers who she was and her disability.

The would-be ballerina came with her drawing that she shared with the performers and the Madam after their dress rehearsal.

You could see in her eye that the attention she was getting was a dream come true for her.

The Madam and would-be ballerina had gotten into a long conversation, which seemed to last for hours. The ambulance driver was getting upset until I told he would get double pay (The extra pay came out of my pocket.).

The intern was flirting with the nurse. I was flirting with the ballerinas all this time telling of my accident and my work. However, just as I was nearing getting a date, the Madam came into the lobby. Madam then order the troupe home and to be ready for the new opening the next night.

I thanked her, as we proceeded to get our would-be ballerina out of the theater, and into the ambulance, as it was snowing.

Our would-be ballerina was so happy for weeks on ends as she told others of her night out and showing the drawings of the performance she did from memory.

About a week or so afterward The Madam would come to visit her on a regular basic until she had our would-be ballerina move in with her. The last I heard our would-be ballerina did costume and set designing for the Madam.

Terminal Ward

I volunteered to be a scoutmaster at Collier Hospital at a special ward for what I called "terminal ward". Most of children, who could not be taken care at home, would live there, a number died there while I was there.

The ward was dreary looking; it had a split colored walls, black and green, with flowers that came from all over New York, funerals homes, conventions, VIP parties and the like. They were supposed to brighten up the place, but the dying flowers were only reflecting the dying taken place on the ward.

Each time I came, I look on the patient status board on the inside staffroom to see whom still alive.

Joey

One child, Joey, an 8-year-old Puerto Rican died on my lap while I was telling a story to the scout troop. When I realized he had stopped breathing, I motioned to the nurse, who told me to finish telling my story to the other children there, while she went to get a gurney and a body bag.

The older children seemed to have known Joey was already dead before I knew it. They seemed to be so use to the dying in the ward. I was not, after the children left for their beds and the nurse and an orderly picked up Joey's lifeless body, I went outside to vomit and cried all night. I even was crying when I left the hospital to go to the nurse's dorm on the island where I lived.

De Pal

De Pal was one of my older scouts, an Explorer Scout. He was a Spinal Bifida and about seventeen years old. I made him my assistant. He was not dying but had lived there a number of years. I could not understand why he was there. It seemed like the courts put him there and forgot him.

A number of years later, while I was about to give a speech in Washington D.C., he came right out of audience to front, near the podium, and turn to the audience.

He claimed that I told him to run away from the hospital. He did and now was working and married.

I did not know he was going to be there, he thank me as the audience applauded as we shook hands (Hook and hand!) and he returned to his place in the audience.

Derrick

When, I was first being show the children ward I came upon two children fight with each other.

One child was about to clobber the other child over the head with his hook. I caught his hook with my hook. His eyes followed his hook to my hook and then to my face and said "I am trouble this time, aren't I!" I replied with "You sure are?"

This was my first meeting with Derrick. We would get to know each other for the next two years before I went into my deep depression or bi-polar lapse after my first wife and broke up.

Derrick was a thalidomide baby, born without any limbs what so ever except small ball-like stumps at shoulders and hips.

He been in this hospital for most of his entire life and had never been outside the hospital not even once to go on a field trip or any outing the hospital had for the other children.

The parent maintained control and custody of Derrick but never ever came to see him or talk to him on the phone. They refused Derrick from ever leaving the hospital, even on field trips.

Derrick had a most sailors' saltiest mouth I ever heard, except the old sailor I knew in my hometown of San Diego. Derrick was tough and demanding; he did what he wanted, short of running the hospital staff but he knew how to manipulate staff to get what he wanted.

However, once I get him into a scout uniform his life changed. I used the uniform to blackmail him to changing his behavior or not wearing his uniform. I once had him stripped of his uniform down to his t-shirt and shorts right in front of his peers and nursing staff when he was really out of line. "You are disgracing the uniform of a scout and I want you to take it off the uniform!" I commanded. He refused. Therefore, I had the nurse and orderly to take off the uniform, they were more than happy to do so because Derrick was just giving them a very bad time too.

Little by little, we came to trust each other and became close buddies. He would refer to me as his "Big buddy".

Through the social worker, we found loopholes in Derrick's medical orders to get Derrick out of the hospital on field trips and eventually to my home every other weekend as part of the medical treatment plan his parent's had signed earlier in his life.

All the reports on Derrick were made to sound, as it was an authorized treatment plan by doctor, who never seems to pay any attention to the reports, just signing off on them. Since the parents were never there to check up on him, they knew nothing of what was going on.

My contract with Derrick was simple, he would wear the artificial arms and legs and walk, about a half a football field, to the waiting Green Limo, that I hired to take him home for the weekends.

He would be about three feet tall without his arms and legs, but he was tall as I was with his limbs on.

At first he would argue he could not make it, cussing at every step of the way but all the patients and staff along the route would edge him on until he finally made it to the "Green" limo.

There he would stand in front of the big limo doors and fall down on to the rear seat, quickly getting out of his hardness and suit he was wearing. He then would jump up on the rear seat facing to rear window sticking his tongue out to all who watched him leave the hospital.

The first time he came to my apartment, he was spell bound, he has never been to a real home. He stayed in the guest room with a big beds with no guardrails, a big sofa to watch TV on, and bathroom with a bidet to wash clean and air-dry our asses, a bathtub to swim in and a personal attendant, Jerry.

I could take anywhere but he wanted to stay at the apartment all the time until one day, we went to the nearby Prospect Park in Long Island. I took him in a wheelchair with his arms and legs on.

While sitting on a park bench and Derrick, sitting next to me in his wheelchair, a gang of black children came by. They looked at us strangely asking what had happen to us, since both of us had no arms and Derrick sitting in the wheelchair with wooden legs showing at the bottom of his pants legs.

I had Derrick tell them but was shy; I prompted him and he told what had happen to him and me. He told them that he lived at a hospital and visited me every other weekend.

They asked many questions then went off to play. They soon came back and asked if they could play with Derrick. I said yes but Derrick was not too sure until I told him he could take his limbs off, which made him more independent. Underneath his limbs and his clothing he had beach shorts and a t-shirt.

After climbing out of his limbs and climbing back into his wheelchair, the boy pushed him to the playground. The boys took turn playing with his wheelchair. They put Derrick in a bucket type swing and took turns pushing him. They played on the marry-go-round and slit on the slide protecting him from the other rough kids.

Afterwards, they followed us home and played with him there until they went home for their dinners.

Two weekends later, they showed up at my apartment with a wagon in tow and asked if Derrick could go play with them. Before I could say anything, Derrick rolled onto the wagon and they were off and running toward the elevator at the Willow Apartment.

It seemed that they were there every time Derrick came home. One time I decide to take Derrick to the movies, he wanted his friend to go too, so we went to each of the boy's apartments nearby and asked their parents if they could go.

Hence, off we went on the subway to a movie house, watch two different movies, and sneak in a third.

I bought each the cokes and popcorn, the boys took turns feed both us, without being asked to do so. They seemed to have an instinct of what needed to been done for us, even taking Derrick to the restroom.

This went on until some state social worker got wind on what we doing. She filed an injunction on me, not to take Derrick out of the hospital again as well as not to let me have access to Derrick.

I went to court with hospital social workers and medical staff members to help plead my case, but the state social had brought in the parent of Derrick, both said that they were going to sue the hospital and move Derrick to an unknown place for him to be protecting from me.

The judge said in closing, saying a severely handicapped person, like myself, could not be able or trusted to take care of another severely handicapped person, "like the blind leading the blind."

I did lose my tempers and told off the state social worker, then soon after told off parent for abandoning him and then judge pound down his gavel so hard, that I think I heard it crack. He order the bailiff to sit me down and said the hearing was over. He would not hear our side of the case. He approved of the State Social worker and then after my outburst, he ordered that I would not allow seeing him, or no talking with him again or even say goodbye to him.

I had been told by the hospital that I could not even work with other children there anymore. They had guards placed at the children ward entrance to keep me from entering again.

One of the hospital social worker did manage to talk to Derrick but he did not understand. I even tried to sneaking a letter to him but it intercepted.

Up until this day, I never knew what happen to him.

The last few weeks there on Welfare Island, I cannot remember well, because I had other girlfriend problems, I slip into a deep depression and had many shock treatments, causing me to forget the finer details of what really happen towards the end of Derrick and our relationship.

What I did tell above is what I think happen or has been told to of what had happened.

Beer to the Rescue

On the men only floor, I made friends with two physical therapist interns from Boston, Mass. that befriended me. They just happen to have the same needs as I had, SEX and we tried to date every good-looking nurse in the building, but we often came out empty handed or empty hooked.

We tried to bring these lovely nurses to our floor but would you know it, there was another Male Nurse "Gretchen" on that floor too.

I had planned an activity with my handicapped scouts, where each asked to write a note about themselves on the back of a postcard with the hospital address printed on the on the top of hospital note pad. They were going to place the not into a clear bottle, then pop on a cork with a little U.S. flag. I was hoping to start a pen pals program outside the Hospital that would write them and become their friends.

The problem then, was to find twelve clear bottles. I spent the afternoon, trying to find clear bottles but only found a few. I told my friends of what I was doing; asking if they had any in their room. Of course, they said they did not because of hospital dorm rules but offer to help me find some. That evening the interns came to my rescue.

We drove off to the nearest bar off the island. We asked the bar tender if he had any clear glass beer bottles, he said no, it was too early in the evening.

Therefore, my friend suggested that the three of us have four bottles each of beer to make up the twelve we needed.

We asked for four bottles each and drunk them as it was our civic duty to have bottles for the kids.

As we got to the end of the twelve bottles, we asked for a bag to put them in. He said he did not have any but would give us a crate to take the empty back to the hospital with but we had to pay for the twelve more bottles plus deposits on all of the bottles we were taking.

Well, we knew we could not take full bottles back to the dorm, so we again all came to the same conclusion, "for the cause!" we would drink the other twelve bottles, making it eight bottles each. We were really getting drunk for "for the cause!", but we were dedicated to get empty bottles for our scouts.

We drove back to our dorm with our faces that was saying, "We were triumph and dedicated men on a mission well done!"

It was late at night. We were loud and we happen to get on one of nurse floor, but no Nurse "Gretchen.

We sneaked around the floor, peeking in keyholes and we lifted one of my friends on my shoulder to view in on a nurse's room from a glass vent window above the doors. Apparently, she heard us and started towards her door. We quickly got him down and quietly as possible ran to hide around the corner of one of halls.

We were trying not to laugh loudly. Nevertheless, I think a numbers of the nurse might have heard us, but fearing getting in trouble with us, they stayed in their rooms.

I said I was going down to my room to piss; however, they wanted me to stay. I said no, and then they pulled my pants down to my ankles so I could not run. They ran to the open elevator and left without me.

Since I could not pull my pant up with my hooks and fearing the old Nurse "Gretchen would find me, I skirted the walls to the elevator. The elevator came up and when the elevator doors open inside were two lovely nurses in their white nurse's uniforms, they giggled as I skirted past them as they came out. I do not know what they were thinking but all sorts of rumors were flying round the two hospitals the next day.

Now I was afraid that the nurse "Gretchen(s)" would be arm to the teeth, the next time.

The Quad and the Sex

While there on Welfare Island, I met a beautiful young adult female, who was a quad. She worked at one at hospital off the island as an information officer but needed respiratory care during the night and had an attendant with her at night to care for her at the nurse dorm.

We became very good friends and started to get romantic. She asked me to go with her to her parent house in upstate New York.

She had to wear a chest respirator at night to help her breath. The parents had fixed a sofa for me next to her bed.

She had me come to her bed and lay next to her while we made out and while she played with my penis, since her hands were still working.

She loved me kissing her neck and face where she could feel. She was an incomplete quad and could feel some other parts of body. She knew, as a man, that I wanted to kiss and suck on her breasts and let me though she had no feeling there. However, she and I knew we could not have intercourse because the high probability of getting an infection in her vagina because she had to use a catheter.

We were really getting into it when the tube to her chest pack came off the chest respirator. It was making a loud, air rushing noise, I was so afraid the sound was loud enough that her parents would hear it. So I put the end to my mouth trying to muffle the noise which was making my lungs expand as the machine connected to it kept going, She was cracking up with laughter as I tried several times to get it back into her chest pack hole with my mouth; I was not wearing my prosthesis at the time.

Finally was able to succeed in plugging air hose back into her chest pack.

I was sweating, as I believe her parent would be in at any moment. They did not, so after a few minutes pasted we went on taking turns at oral sex slowly on each other, me playing outside through her panties until we or I climaxed. She said she think she climaxed too, because she felt she getting hot, sweaty and then return to normal body temperature.

The last I heard, she got married to another Quad, a patient at the same hospital where she worked.

Food Poising

Nine medical staff died at Long Island Welfare Hospital from food poising and many more of us required hospitalizations. The general patient population was not effect, just those who ate at the staff or doctor lounges. They closed both lounges until they were able to find the source. (I cannot remember what the source was.)

A special staff sub-ward was setup with-in one of medical floor for the non-critical patients, like me.

We were very sick with high fevers and suffered severe abdominal pains.

Even the patient themselves pitch in whenever they could, bring water, packaged foods and helped clean up the vomiting that that ran rampant on sub-ward.

Many doctors including military medical personnel from all over the city of New York came in.

Patients, staff members and my volunteers from both hospitals came to see me, including many from the nurse's dorm; even some of the Nurse "Gretchen(s)" came to see me.

Child Dies on Glue

One time I befriended a group of children on the street, 5-12 year olds boys and girls, who lived by themselves, in a vacant apartment across the street from my apartment.

First, they were asking for a handout of money, then food. Then one very cold winter night, New York was freezing over, they ask could they spent the night at my apartment to keep warm.

I called the welfare department, but did not help us. They said they too many children in the like of this situation and have ran out of resources, but would give me a stipend if I would care for them during the winter storm crisis.

I could not get to work either, transportation was at a standstill, trash was not being pickup, police could not get to us and fire trucks could not get any water from the frozen fire hydrants. Consequently, like a camp counselor, we made the best of things.

They told me that they were not going back to the welfare department because they sent them to orphanages or foster homes that were interest in the money; they got for having them but did little to care for them.

Then one day they disappeared. Maybe fearing the Welfare Department would come for them.

Sometime early spring, they brought a lifeless body of one of their own to my place. I called for an ambulance, but there was nothing the paramedics could do for the boy.

They again spent the night with me. They wanted me to help them with burying arrangements. They knew it would be a pauper funeral; they wanted me to be there so the authority would think they were with me.

While they waited for the funeral, I called one of the doctors from the City Morgue, who I met, as he would come to our hospitals to pick up the patients who have died there.

He told me that the child had died from lung suffocation due to glue sniffing which crystallize the inside surface of the lung.

I asked him if I could bring the children over to see the lung, in hopes of getting them to stop using glue to get them high on.

They next day I gathered as many as the dead boy's friends as I could find. On the premise, that they would be a "viewing of the boy's body" for the children.

We took a subway to the morgue. While waiting to view the body in a lab, the doctor brought in the lung that already cut open and it showed why the child died.

Some were, I believe were being affecting by the showing, while others were too hardened to life; they showed no emotion what so ever.

Afterwards they brought in the boy's body, they stood around as some cried and said their goodbyes.

Only the group that had stayed with me during the winter came to the funeral.

I never seen them again, except, maybe one in the news that also died from glue sniffing.

The Handicapped Foundation for New York

I found an additional job at The Handicapped Foundation for New York as a group worker. My job was to work with young handicapped adult with recreational and socializing activities.

They were very bright, some were working, others were in college and others were in vocational training programs.

The social skills they needed were not much as the Director said they would need.

They lack skills in planning social get together and/or organized club events. These activities were often done for them and had no skills in carryout these events by themselves.

My four steps in making them more independent were simple:

- First, I would show them what good activities and social event were like.
- Secondly, I would show them how to organize and carry out different types of activities and social events.
- Thirdly, I would watch them put on activities and social events by themselves.
- Fourthly, if I did my job well, I was not around to help them, guide them or even advise them on their major club activities.
- They were on their own and me without a job.

Personal Philosophy:
"I teach you!—We will do together! I will watch you do! Then I am gone".

When I did any activities or social event, I try cutting the activity at its highest point of enjoyment or fun. If they wanted more, they had to help in planning and participate in execution of activities and social event.

Then I would watch them do the planning and participating in execution of social activities and events. I would only advise them when needed and stress any safety concerns I observed.

The forth is where many group workers, social workers, recreation leaders, recreational therapists and rehabilitation personnel fail at in truly making a disabled person independent. **"They need to do on their own!"** Too many in these professions, have their patients, clients or members dependant on them for everything, having the same group without their involvement in their activities.

Our rehabilitation services are just revolving doors; they serve the same patients, clients or members, year after year in their agency.

Imagine if everyone in their group became independent, they would soon be out of a job. That I why believe every job in these fields should have a limited contracts with a bonus given if they succeeded in developing independence for they patients. There will always be more new clients out there than they can possibly work with.

For many non-profit agencies and organizations, it is nothing more than job for the executives, many who happen to be paid as much as CEOs in private industries, having many time more employees than the non-profit agencies and organizations has.

No Joy Ride for Professional Disabled

Working for handicapped agencies is no joy ride for disabled professional employees.

Many disabled service agencies hire disabled as P. R., but often isolated and not invited into the real inter-working of their agency or into the social life of other able-body employees.

At this job, there was a staff member who left a staff meeting because of this author was at meeting. Before he left, he said this to the members of this meeting group, "How can I talk about disabled clients freely, I feel uncomfortable when another disabled person is working alongside me in these meetings. I have to watch that I don't say anything to offend this person (me)"

Bear Mountain

The Boat trip up the Hudson to Bear Mountain was probably the biggest climax event for my group in the whole year.

They decided to go to Bear Mountain, an island near West Point. I did nothing but show up for trip.

They figured since the able-bodies (non-disabled) did not have to pre-plan with Boat Company were coming, neither were they.

About twenty-two or so disabled young adults showed up un-announced. Some in wheelchairs, some on crutches, canes and ambulatory walking cerebral palsies, polios and just cripples, like me, came for the trip.

Most were there early before departure, with their backpacked, blankets and of course, ice chests, which they handed over to the crew who searched for counter ban, like liquor or pot, which they could have hidden it their blanket or underneath their wheelchair or tote bags. If they were to bring them, they would hide them inside the tubes of the canes, crutches and wheelchairs.

Then just as the boat had just started to leave, two of our late comers came; one Crip threw one of his crutches onto the ship deck and pole-vaulted onto the deck with his other crutch. The other crazy Crip took a flying leap on to the ship rails, almost losing his grip with his good hand but a deck hand and a few passengers help catch him in time and pull him over the rails onto the deck. He could had easily fallen in, Boy, if he did fell into the water, I would never work in this field again.

The ship captain was not too pleased; he asked who was in charge. Each pointed to each other in succession ending with me, I then pointed to the most severely disabled in the group who had planned the trip.

In discussed manner, not saying a word, the captain turned and charged up a stairs leading to his wheelhouse on the boat.

As the ship or boat cruised up the Hudson, the gang of "Capthooks", they liked to call themselves, runs all over the ship, buying snacks, sodas and souvenirs.

Grabbing their own corner of the ship near front, they tried their lung out to sing old seafaring songs, when they ran out of those, they started with camp songs, then startup an old type Hootenanny sing-along with a number of other passenger joining in.

However, when we started to pass West Point, they started sing military hymns. As they seen the flying colors of big red, white and blue flying over the Academy they stop. Dianne, our best singer in our group began singing "America the Beautiful" then the gang and then whole ship passengers and crew sang with her. That moment, our group won the respect of both passengers and crew, including the captain.

I followed with "This Land is Your Land". I have a good singing voice too!

When we got o the island and unloaded, the gang looked up the big steep hill they would have to climb to get to the picnic grounds on top of the hill. It would take most of the morning for most of the gang to get up there. However, being the gang of Capthooks, they saw a solution. Near the dock was a firehouse for the whole island, one fire truck with an ambulance to boot. They talked to the fire chief and got themselves up the hill on top of the fire truck, with some hanging out back of the fire truck and in the ambulance with them being allowed to using the lights and sirens.

I had to walk up the hill as not to involve my agency nor directly get paid for the trip, if someone got hurt.

It was a nice day; the gang organized a wheelchair and ambulatory flag football game with the able-body(s) who were well drunk. There were lots of injures with able-bodies being ran over by wheelchair and tripping over crutches and canes.

We were short on hamburgers and paper plates but neighbors on the hill pitch in. When the beer run low, one of the able-body drag one of the gang off his wheelchair, went to the park store and bought three cases of beer and bag of beer drinking cups.

By day's end you could not tell who, was handicapped or just plain drunk, as they came down the hill to the docks.

On board coming back, you could not tell apart our gang from the rest of the passengers, either the gang blended in with them or the passenger blended in with the gang.

By the time, we reached New York City, everyone, the gang and passengers, who lived in or near the city, were making plans for another outing.

I just disappeared into the street, knowing my job had ended with at The Handicapped Foundation for New York.

—Thanks for the opportunity,

CHAPTER 8

Meeting the Russians

Travel Plans to Russia

When I got to England's Heathrow Airport, I transfer to a Russian Airline to Moscow without a layover, then another Russian aircraft to a airport outside the City, which I still cannot pronounce it. (Let's see, I have it here in this computer under an Excel file named "Travel plan to Russia",) Ok it is in the town of Fryazino, 35 miles from Moscow) to meet a welcoming delegation from the Russian Hospital,

Checkpoint

I had troubles passing the customs checkpoint. My suitcases were thoroughly gone over.

Besides my clothing, many of my items that were ADL (Aids to Daily Living) helping devices and a heavy bag full of my driving equipment, which they never seem to have never seen before. I had to explain each item to them.

That was follow by having them taking off my suit coat to check my artificial limbs, this I could understand with all the smuggling go on in Russia.

Then they wanted to check my computer bag and they turn on my laptop on to check the content of my drives. I use two memory 500 GB sticks and they wanted to check each one for banned content. I did not think they could read any of it, but maybe looking for pornographic material on my computer.

I hid my adult entertainment file under a data file subfolder because it would be too long to check all the folders inside that folder. But when they got to my nudist camp pictures they called their superior. He looked, noticing they were not pornographic in nature or was a nudist himself, told the guards to disregard their findings. Russia has a large number of nudist "naturalist" colonies and groups.

About the same time, my interpreter and the hospital director, whom been waiting a long time, finally came to the checkpoint. They asked questions and they got the attention of the same superior I was taking to earlier.

After a brief discussion and showing papers, the superior rushed over to the guards and told them to repack my belonging while he escorted me back to the director and interpreter.

Meeting the Translator

As soon as I reached them, she was apologizing for the superior and his men. With the superior nodding his head as if he just apologized himself.

She was very formal in the introduction of the Hospital Director, noting his position and his responsibility of the hospital and of me from a printed paper.

After the formalities, she then introduced me to our driver, who was transporting us to the directly to hospital. He seemed apprehensive as he was puzzled on how to shake my hook.

My assigned interpreter just straight forward translator, that director said or said to me from the hospital limo driver while he was loading my stuff into the trunk of the limo.

There were words in her translations I did not understand. Maybe they were titles, places or things, or were too fast for me to understand the translation of them.

Meeting the Hospital Director

The director was cordial, and but an utterly cold person. He gave me papers that I could not read or understand except that they seem to be official papers with stamped seals embossed to them. I failed to have them interpreted all the time I was in Russia.

We stood together at the airport while the driver received my belongings from the guards on a cart.

The director said very little but kept side glancing at my hooks.

Long Limo Ride to Hospital

It was very cold outside but there was a heater blowing inside the car. It felt good because I did not put my suit coat back on to keep me warm, which I am sure, puzzled the driver.

The interpreter started to describe the high points of our drive with tourist guide like precision. She later told me she was a tour guide in St. Petersburg before going to school to become an official interpreter for the government.

CHAPTER 9

The Hospital

Seeing Hospital for First Time

Everything seemed gray as we drove through the village and on to a country road leading to this huge hospital compound.

A short distance from the hospital I could hear jets taking off and a tarmac extension leading nearer the hospital. They told me it was a Russian Air Force Base.

The compound buildings were all red bricked with white trims between floors. From the base of the buildings reached about three stories high.

They pointed out the employee dorm that appeared like it was six floors high, while I was thinking that where I be staying.

There seemed to be lots of trees and shrubs on walkways and in-between buildings. There seemed be no flowers blooming, maybe is getting too cold for them to be growing here.

The grounds looked very clean and organized. I am almost sure this is the way it is always kept or maybe because I was coming.

The limo first stopped at the Director's residents, the driver step out to open his door. Sensing the director was going to tell me something, he just stood at the door of the limo until he seen the director move towards the door and then open it.

The director said through my interpreter to have a good dinner and rest.

He also said when I was ready, meaning as soon as I recover from the jet lack, which I was supposed to have, I would be given a complete tour of the hospital and meet the key staff.

Then we drove to a smaller residential looking building close to the administration building.

Again the driver had jumped out quickly as he seen me moving towards the door to open it. He opened the door motioning to my interpreter to come out then motioned me. She was sitting across from me, I was going to give her a hand or hook to help her out but he beat me to it. It seems to be the same protocol, everywhere we went.

As we entered the residence, you could feel the warm heat rushing at us to warm our cold bodies, well as least mine.

There was not an audience to greet me except the housekeeper. She showed my interpreter and me straight to our rooms, saying that whenever I was ready, she would call all the key staff of the resident together and introduce me to each of them.

I asked her if there was a possibility of meeting the key staff during dinner that evening but she informed me that they have already planned to meet me at the hospital meeting room the next day after my tour of the hospital.

Again, my interpreter was no help in getting across the idea that I wanted to meet them more informally than they had planned.

The housekeeper interrupted me, to ask me if I wanted to have my lunch brought to my room or have it in the dining room. I was tired and thinking it would be a sandwich with no one to place it and balance it on top of my hook. So in this case I told her I would have it in my room. Where, I could directly eat my meal from the plate, much like a dog eating from a plate. I did not want to embarrass myself just yet in my new setting.

CHAPTER 10

My Residence

The resident inside was much larger from than I expected and my office or work room was large. The room came with: work desk for my computer; lot of shelves space; a modern looking television set with DVD and a video player; sofa with a blanket and pillow holders underneath the end tables attach to it; a big picture painted to look like a window showing the countryside, a large walking in closet; plus a private bath and shower, a toilet with a electric bidet attachment that they order for me, as I requested from them.

I did not know if my room was typical as the others were, as I never did ventured into other resident rooms.

Amenities

There were neither recreational facilities nor a swimming pool. There might of had have been somewhere on the ground but I was not never made aware on them. Maybe, they thought I could not swim. However, I could swim and did some diving with my son, when he became a certified diver in San Diego, when I was much younger and active.

I was thinking that I would see other staff members who lived there also but they were all at the hospital or at the administration building. I did not see anyone else there at night for nearly a week except my attendants and my interpreter. Later I found out there were others, as I adjusted my hours to meet theirs, I started to see more of them at meal times, but I still felt isolated.

House Staff

There was not a cheerful face on any of house staff members.

They all wore the same color uniforms, a dull gray. The head mistress wore a ruffed blouse and the man in charged wore a bow tie and jacket. All the other men in the household staff wore just a pair of black pants and white shirt with a bow tie.

The staff seemed to be there night and day. I learned later, that is because of the low salary, they worked double shifts.

I never did get to know any of them personally except for one of my attendant/nurse (Care Giver) who I got to know very personally.

At first, they seemed to have made mental notes on how I like things and what I would eat.

Anything that required to be cut for me became how it was served, mouth sized.

My breads came buttered and in the mornings, the jelly was added on my toast for me.

I did not like hot drinks, so my drinks were cold, sometime with ice. Even my hot chocolate drinks were served ice cold like carton chocolate milk drinks at home.

When I first came to meals I would bring along a straw, soon they had a straw at each meal or lunch they brought to my office.

What I really liked was the ceramic dish wear, they were heavy and I did not have to have a glass full of water to push against, like plastic or paper plates. There were also real cloth napkins.

The one thing I could not figure out was the fact that no matter what time I came down or came in they would be ready to serve me a hot meal.

If I had stayed in my office, my lunch would be brought in without me requesting it.

If on road trips, there seem to be a completely hot meal that would be taken out of the trunk of the limo complete with a folded table and chairs to sit outside.

A table was attached to the rear of the front seats, if it too cold. After they served us, the drive and my attendant would sit on the front seats with a window or partition closed to give us privacy, like I needed it, with my cold interpreter.

I was never short on laundry, it seem they washed my clothes as soon as I took them off.

My room ways always ready, even if I left for a short time, it was ready as if I was never been there before.

I even check to see if there were cameras or if a staff member was hiding in the closet or if there was a secret door at which they watched my comings and goings, I found nothing.

Feeling of Unwelcome or Coldness

I was not surprised by the new situation, but felt that, I was coldly received; it was a feeling of being in a foreign country unable to communicate or be trusted.

I am used to setting the tone when I come in to a new situation, now they were setting the tone. It was coldness and remained that way until I left the hospital.

My Care Giver/Attendant/Nurse

She young, good-looking, but not sexy looking in Russian nurse's uniform. I think she had reached eighteen and I thought to myself. "If she going to bathes me, I am going to be in trouble."

The first few times she bathes me, she had no response to my penis-erecting while she washed it.

Then she seem to take more time washing my penis, by the end of my first week on our tour, she washed until I came.

I realized she was not getting paid very well as my care giver or attendant, so I started paying her a tip.

One time, she got wet from the shower head turned the wrong way. I could make out her braless breast and I let her know it.

She grinned as if she meant me to see them. I believe she knew I wanted more sexual favors.

The next morning she just opened her uniform blouse showing her nude breast to me.

Getting the hint, I increased the tip.

Sure enough she not only showed her breasts, she not wearing no underwear under her uniform, she was binding down to exposed her ass and making sure I seen her vagina, then she turned and proceeding to jack me off while she was soaping my body.

I added more to her daily rubles; she would undress and gave me a shower naked.

I wondered how far she would, so I added more rubles. This time she added by giving me an oral treatment.

I again added more. She came into shower this time, her body pressing mine, with her hand holding my penis as she rubbed it on the surface of her vagina.

Well, you already know what we did next after I added more rubles.

Each morning and evening we had brief sex until I climaxed, then she wiping my penis dry she would go about her business caring for me . . . shaving me, dressing or undress me and making sure, I got my ADDH and diabetes medication and injection of insolents, as well as monitoring my blood sugars during the day.

She would come to the office twice a day to see if needed to be helped to go to the restroom.

She never said a word during these encounters.

I was feeling real contended with her for about a month or so. However, for some reason she was replaced with an old hag.

Maybe they found out what we were doing or she made enough rubles to quit.

I never seen her again, nor did I paid the old hag a tip.

CHAPTER 11

The Tour of the Hospital

The housekeeper again informed me that the key staffs would be awaiting me at the main hospital's administration meeting room after the hospital and ground tour.

There was a young woman, all bundled up, standing near the main door outside the dining room. Her eyes seemed curious but very formal as we approached. I said hi to her, followed by my interpreter translation and her nodding her head, as she understood and opening a huge door to a room where people hang their coats and kept their boots or galoshes.

My interpreter donned her overcoat then they waited to see if I was going to donned mine. I nodded no and proceeded to go out the door into the cold air.

My artificial arms kept most of my upper body warm; while my lower body did seem to feel the very cold air outside.

They seemed pretty bundle up in their coats and hats. It was not until I got into the first warm building that I felt my ears lopes were freezing and in pain.

The Ground and Buildings

The first that impressed me was how clean and organized was the hospital complex.

The streets and walkways between the buildings were clean in-spite of the many 10 to 20 foot trees all over the grounds of the complex. It seems that these grounds were always maintained well.

Nowhere did I see a street cleaner machine or signs posted to keep the ground clean. The ground looked as they were swept by hand not by street cleaners, maybe by some of the patients themselves.

I did notice there was a small numbers of street sign used.

Each building had a large building number painted at each corner of the buildings. Each hospital building had a Russian name to it, but our tour guide referred to them by the numbers on the side of the building.

The pavements were a darkish gray like cement. This could have been from the dark overcast that lingers for most of the time that I was there.

The order of the building were simple, the whole hospital complex had been built around the administrative building, but with building number five and six, it seemed to have been built later than the others, maybe as an add on.

The Auxiliary Building and the Grounds

There are a supply warehouses; and a garage building, for their own repair of their vehicles; these were on the outside streets at the rear of the hospital complex.

A large staff dorm seemed to be further away to one side of the complex, while my residential building was much closer to the administration building.

A large kitchen facility stood to the rear of administration building with lot of food carts standing inside being loaded but the interesting thing was the this building seem to be lower than the other buildings.

We were told that there were tunnels leading to each building, even the service buildings. They said it was easier to deliver food in the wintertime yet they preferred to use the ramps that lead to the surface walkways to all the buildings when possible, because the tunnels were not well ventilated, the heat from the food and food warmer made it humid inside the tunnels.

We did not see what being made, but could smell the odors of food being cooked.

We were not there for lunch, to see how the patients were all being feed.

We walked for about less than a mile around the hospital complex before we entered into the first hospital-type building.

I was told the each hospital building housed patients by age group as each group required more care as they grew.

Building 1

The same young lady who met us at my residency door, took my interpreter's coat. Then our young escort had disappeared; I did not even notice that she had left us.

The smell of cleanliness of the hospital was the first thing I noticed.

The hospital inside seemed even larger than they looked from the outside, with offices towards the front and halls leading to wards.

We were led to a meeting room near the offices, which I think is use as a lounge room as well, we were met by key staff members that already knew we were coming, greeted us.

They all stood up as we entered. Each was introduce to me with their full name, their position and responsibilities. My interpreter only translated their position and responsibilities for me, as their all their names would remain the same for me.

After the last one was introduce, that they sat down in unison. It seemed that they all knew why I was there for.

The supervisor of Building 1 explains what ages and the general types of disabilities in these wards of the hospital building we were in.

This building housed on all floors, were both severely disabled and retarded babies from a few day olds to 1 year olds are together.

My interpreter had a hard time finding a translation to describe some of the disabilities in English.

What I gathered that it wound up to mean that these babies in were in a "vegetated state" and all they do was to keep them alive.

"Just here to care for them, as best as we possibly can!" The supervisor said.

There was a feeling of un-welcome-nest or coldness and a somber mood about the staff. No one smiled, or spoke except the supervisor.

When she finishes the introduction to her building purpose and mission, they all rose as if a cue was given them without me knowing it.

The supervisor then got up and motioned us to the door; the staff remained standing without a goodbye gesture as I nodded my head to say thank you.

The halls had shinning wooden floors. It gave a warmth look to the rest of the hospital.

As we walk down the hall I felt their uneasiness of their staff meeting of an American, or it could been my football harness look of my limbs and my hooks or even my brown Mexican skin. It did not seem to be the any of the two possibilities above. Their eyes did not seem to be focus on my arms; I just felt it was maybe more because of the cold war period or distrust of Americans. However, I had no idea or facts to rely on.

The halls lead us to a wing of the hospital that had two big wards at the end of each hall, which split into two wards.

As a whole the hospital building seemed to housed about 300 infants, a 100 per floor, 25 five to a ward, give or take a few.

Some of the babies seem to be, in pre-natal cribs that were donated to them, but they seemed to be too mature for them to be prenatal babies as I have seen in those cribs used before.

The other babies on second floor were in plastic tub like cribs, with rubber mats inside. They were line up straight some with monitors, some of the babies were on IV bottles, others with tubes in their nose and many just seemed lying lifeless.

Baby weighting scales were in each ward, which seems, aside with feeding them, to be the main activities of the nurses there besides taking vitals and changing diapers.

The staffs in these institutions are called "cleaners", the meaning of in Russian and it is clear that children are being cared for, but only in the sense of custodial care.

The older babies were on their tummies with little movement or attention from the cleaners.

As we finish tour the building, we were met by the same girl, who brought us to Building 1. She seems to appear from nowhere.

She took us to the next building without grabbing their coats. I think it was a short walk, no enough time to get cold.

Building 2

The supervisor of Building 2 met us, who lead us to a meeting room much like the first.

Again, the same routine as the staff stood until the last introduction.

There were the same feeling of unwelcome or coldness and somber mood.

The supervisor included a little bit difference data and information.

They also served both severely disabled and retarded babies from 1 year olds to 4 year olds.

The hospital was layout much like the first one, three floors and had the same size wards.

Again, I missed the cue given to the staff before they stood up as we were lead from the meeting of the staff of Building 2.

This hospital building housed about the same as the first: 300 toddlers, a 100 per floor, four wards to each floor and each housed 25 five to a ward.

As a whole the babies were little much bigger and a little heavier than the first babies we seen before.

These had many more cribs, like a regular wooden type with rails on each side. But there were some tub looking ones and a few pre-natal type cribs with some made the children look no bigger than the ones in Building 1.

Again, some of the babies were on IV bottles, others with tubes in their nose and many just lying lifeless.

Baby weighting scales were again like the metal basket type in each of the wards, which also seems again to be the main activities of the nurses.

There was a kind of a ceramic basin in each ward where the babes taken to be washed and a diaper changing table with cabinet full of cloth diapers and baby size t-shirts that covered most of the body. It looked more an assembly lines, as babies and cleaner lined waiting to use the basin. They could have used two more basins, to speed the process.

We finish Building 2 and would you believe, that the same girl met us, she again seems to appear from nowhere.

She took us to the next building, again without grabbing their coats, which I thought were left at Building 1.

It was a little longer walk, but not enough time to get cold as it was from Building 1 to Building 2.

Building 3

The supervisor of Building 3 met us, who lead us to a meeting room, again, much like the first.

Again, the same routine as the staff stood until the last introduction.

There again were the same feeling of unwelcome or coldness and somber.

The supervisor again included a little bit different data and information.

Again as like the first and second, I missed the cue given the staff before they stood up as we started our tour.

They also served both severely disabled and retarded but they were toddlers from 5 year olds to 7 year olds.

This hospital building was different from the last: it housed about 150 or fewer toddlers in total with the same layout and by different types of abilities level, depending more on what type of movement abilities they had.

One ward had toddlers who were sedate or showed little movement, a good number lying on their tummies, quite for the most part, with a few making some type of noise.

Across the hall from the first one ward we seen in that building, toddlers at least have more movement, cried and making all sorts of untellable noise.

The last two wards had toddlers with much more movement, some were trashing back and forth, some were standing, and some were lying down but making lots of noise. A few had restrains to keep the toddlers from climbing out of their cribs.

As we observed the children on the second floor, first we entered the last two wards in the end of the hall, we observed ambulatory toddler, sitting or walking around on top of blue mats in a small glass enclosure. Next to enclosure was their room where they slept at night full of babies' cribs, but metal type cribs beds.

Toward the first ward of the third floor, one on the left side, are the ward for sever cerebral palsy, brain damaged, artistic and Rye syndromes in cribs, some on mats other restraint to their wheelchair or padded titled chairs.

I could not get any of their attention, even when I was making funny faces at them. None seems to know even our presence in the ward.

The second ward on this floor seemed to be for children with severe medical care problem. The ward was much sedate children with cribs and small beds with children on respirators, some more on IV bottles and tubes in their noses. A few more were on monitors with leads were taped up to their bodies.

The smell was more like intensive care room in American hospitals.

As we went to exit the hospital, there again, we were met by the same girl, she again seems to appear from nowhere.

She took us to the next building, again my interpreter and guides without their coats.

It was a little longer walk, still not enough time to get cold.

Building 4

Meeting Building 3 Staff was almost exactly like the rest we visited.

The same size ward, however the beds are the bigger

Mostly physically disabled and subdued children, no mention of the retarded children in this hospital 4.

Some on IV bottles along their beds.

They used a platform weighting scale, where the nurse is holding child are weighted together

Here the children had combed hair and cleanly dressed children

In another ward, we observed children who appear to be four to five years of age. The Nurse told us that their records show them to be eight to ten years old.

Upstairs, we witnessed other children barely able to sit up or crawl— or just learning to do so—whose are reportedly in the age range of eight to ten years old too.

Rhythmic motion or "rocking" is common in these lying down rooms. I noticed that these children were deprived of any form of human contact or stimulation than any of the other wards, except for the cleaner feeding and washing their bodies in a washroom stall with rubber hoses.

Meeting with a Bright Blue Eyed Child

On the third floor, the children in this ward seem about ten years old. As I walk by and glancing at each bed, each child had the same look, each seemed to be in a vegetable like stage, they were non-communicated, starring in no real direction or even making eye contact. However, one boy does make eye contact with me.

He, blinks his eyes at me, I blink back. Then he blinks only one eye, then I blink one eye back at him, we played together for a few minutes with our eyes.

He had a very beautiful smile; his blue eyes seem to tell me that he wanted to communicate with me.

His ward nurse said though my interpreter, that the child was abandon, has been here for most of his life, that all testing showed he had no facial or communicating skills what so ever, no other body movements were ever detected in testing, but was loved because he was so cute.

However, as I was being ushered to go on the see the rest of the ward, but my mind said that this boy could communicate.

Another staff member stated, as we walking to Building 4, that the blinking is auto reflex, he is not communicable, that he been tested as unable to communicate. I wanted to rebut, but it was my first observation of the boy.

Meeting With Nurse Lendorma and Her Child

As we were heading to the exit of Building 4, a nurse who was introduced during the staff introductions approached us.

In Russian, she started to talk to me directly but soon realize I did not understand a word she said. She then turned to my translator, as she spoke to her she kept turning her head toward me. I sensed whatever she was saying was important for her to communicate with me.

Thru the interpretation she said she was one of the nurses here but also a mother of one the children on this ward and that her name was Nurse Tatiana Lendorma.

She pointed to one of the cribs about three rows from where we were standing. She motioned us to follow her to the crib of her child.

The Nurse guiding us was very much like <u>Nurse Ratched</u> from the movie "One Flew Over the Cuckoo's Nest". My pet name for her as the "Cold Nurse", which I had lots of runs ins with her since my office was next to her. She thought I was too loud in my voice and disturbed her concentration and said so in a few of my contacts. She was not very diplomatic about it either. Once she march into my office and signaled with her finger to her lips to shut up.

The "Cold Nurse" who was giving us the tour seemed a bit perturbed that the nurse/mother had even approached us but did follow us to the crib.

Nurse Lendorma introduced us to her son Sergei, who lied there motionless unaware our present or his mother.

She stated that this place was very important in the care of her vegetable like son and help keeping her son alive and he was very important for her daughter's future.

She started to continue but "Cold Nurse" who was conducting our tour broke in on her conversation with us, we had to move on to next building, adding in Russian, that the other building's staff was waiting on us. Nurse Lendorma seemed that she had more to say but quickly added as she walk away with her head bowing down ". . . please help keep this place going for my daughter sake". She then added "The work they do here can save my daughter, please don't kill her too!" With her last words to me, her eye swelled with tears as she tried to wipe them dry as she headed back to her station.

I was stung by her remarks!

I had hoped that my interpreter knew what she was talking about. When I asked her, she nodded no with a face of puzzlement too.

I want to follow up with her on that she just said, but I could not because the "Cold Nurse" gave her a very strong look of disapproval at Nurse Lendorma, this time with her lips puffed up.

Therefore, I left, as not to antagonize the "Cold Nurse" again toward Nurse Lendorma, hoping to catch her later without the "Cold Nurse" presence.

As we left, the "Cold Nurse" was giving Nurse Lendorma real look of disapproval.

The "Cold Nurse" pointed us back to exit, saying as she exiting us, that there was never any hope for Nurse Lendorma son, Sergei or for her daughter.

I was thinking, as I exited Building 4, that this mother was distraught over her son but by being here he was being take of care and the reference to her daughter, was that she could not financially support her the for future or needed an increase in her salary, thou she never stated anything of the kind?

I was hoping for any kind of response or comments from my translator, but not a word came from her mouth as we walked to the next build.

You guessed it right, the same girl met us.

Building 5

I received the same feelings, like the rest, the feeling of unwelcome or coldness and somber as well as the uneasiness of meeting of an American.

The staff meet was almost the same, but one nurse did smile at me. Nevertheless, I missed the cue once again.

In this building it look as that was a just a job, no holding, caring or talking to the children.

Feeding them, taking temps, weighting, clean from bowl moments and charting but some, about a third, have little no combing of hair or recent shaving of face.

Same size ward but the beds are full size non-electrical hospital but half about the numbers of patients than in Building 1.

All seem to be about the same size and weight

Some still on IV bottles, some naked, being washed. All of their bodies did showed evidence of many corrective or medical surgeries

Two are on respirators, the old iron lung type.

Here the nurse weights patents and were lifted on a sling from the bed to the a weight scale gurneys

In asking why the numbers, the supervisor said it was because they were of teenage age and heavier that why the number is smaller.

But after the tour of the last hospital building I did not like their reasoning, something seemed wrong. We observed that there was less number of patients in some buildings but it emptier of patients as we went hospital building to fifth hospital building. Are not the same numbers moving from building to building as they get older?

I asked if some of the patients in other building being transferred to other facilities, there was no response, maybe I insulted her by asking the question.

Building 6

Same O, Same O
Everything was as the same as the last with the staff.
Same size building but large rooms with glassed fitting window lined the halls to observe many patients inside.
This where the adult size patients are houses, mostly severely disabled and retarded lived and some were barely ambulatory.
In another ward, each room seem to have around certain size and tallness of patients and very noisy with grunts, yelling and hitting the walls or floor from some of the patients.
Instead of beds, there are twin bed sized blue mats and there was an area for patient's hosing down station in each room. (I was thinking back at one of the summer camps I worked in the states, were doing the same thing.)
Again some naked bodies being washed showed evidence of many corrective or medical surgeries
Weight scales are in a separated room, where nurse weighted the patents and gave out medications
On the top floor of this build were a medical ward and surgery rooms, this building was nearer to the air base tarmac, that I notice coming into the complex of my first day here. I was intrigued with the idea of later watching soviet aircrafts as aviation was of a hobby and great interest of mine.
Sorry but you get no points for this one, the girl was there again but this time she had the overcoats, hats, boots and galoshes were there waiting for us that we brought to Building 1.
I had to stop "second guessing" these Russians. No wonder there was a "Cold War"; we could not out guess them.

CHAPTER 12

Administration Meeting

My Opening Bombed

There seem to be no noise in the administration building just our own footsteps bouncing from the walls.

I was led into a large meeting room with twenty or more people who stood up without a queue and then my interpreter introduced me formally to them.

A luncheon was being served and small talks ensued but I did not understand most of the conversation going on. My interpreter was eating and I did not to disturb her eating because she would be interpreting all afternoon.

I was led to a podium with a table and chair next to it. I expected someone there to welcoming and introduce me to the staff but everyone just waited for me to start the meeting.

I gave them my personal introduction and my "Need for Information" speech.

I was trying to think of some icebreaker, to tell some type of joke.

I realized that most were looking at my hooks, so I went to my old standby joke, "I can tell that it's really cold here when I can feel it in my hooks!" My translator translated but it bombed.

Administration Staff Introduces Themselves

As the Public Relation man for the hospital, I introduce my role and their cooperation needed in getting information that I will need to have to accomplish my mission.

Then I asked my interpreter if each one would introduce themselves and tell me their administrative position was on the staff.

Each person stood up one by one as it seemed prepared as if they knew that I was coming.

Some of the positions were the ambiguous and the interpreter used what I thought was outdated titles and duties. However, as I explored each person positions I realized that they were still operating in the time zone that, I first worked in a state hospital system forty years ago.

I was trying to find something in their descriptions that I could relate to and begin a conversation but again my interpreter was of no help.

As we got to the last person, I realized that, everybody was seated according to rank and status among the staff.

I tried fishing around a little, trying to find anyone who spoke English. There seem to be only five people who responded but most said they knew very little.

One young lady in the back said she had been to English speaking school in Moscow and had conversations with Americans there. I replied to her "I'm glad I'm not going to be talking to the walls only while I am here." There was a little bit of a smile on her face and others as interpreter translated.

Help Write Bio Info Card

I then told them that I wanted them to write a small biographic data and a short job description just like the one they had given me in their introduction.

The interpreter was just as a puzzle as were the audience in my statement. They all seem to have the look on their face as if to say, "If you don't know, who does? Is that your job" There was a delay until interpreter was done, except for the young lady in the back room who smiled again while I waited.

I had hoped that someone knew what I was supposed up to do there.

"My job as a Public Relationship person is to make this hospital and you to look good." I told them forcibly.

However as I was talking, I was felt that they did not know what Public Relationship was in the first place.

I then proceeded to tell them what I was my experience, hoping to light up a face or two to help me set a direction for my talks. There was not anything I said for them to relate to; they seem to be very even more puzzled as well as I went along.

I then explained that I wanted to spend the days looking over the facilities and in each of their departments. I told them "I was going to try to understand your department as much as I can possibly learn."

"Then I tried a different angle. "I need you and each of you to be less informal with me. I will be less informal with you. I am an informal type of guy". That bombed too!

Public Relationship

"I want to know not only about your job, you duties, your mission but also most importantly I want to get to know you. Why are you here? Why you entered the field or profession? What do you want to do differently or change?

"Public Relationship is more than just putting out press releases, but to capture the spirit of this hospital and also the spirit of the people who work here, who really make this hospital what it is.

The best Public Relationship tool is you, making sure to the public you are the most important tool in making this hospital and your work here well known to your people and the world.

In reverse the public would know what could be done to help you do your work, make it better or make it more fun?

I know what you will be tell me is you would like to see a better salary. I do not know if I could do anything about it but I will try." There were a few smiles in the group.

"I will speak openly about my job, my public relations duties and my goals with you. I hope you will do the same."

Becoming Disabled

"As for my disability, I have no problem in discussing that with you in a group or in a one to one conversation.

I have spent Over 61 years with my disability and over 44 years working with the disabled.

Each of you eventually will have a disability, you will have to deal with it, and you will have to accept or reject your disability.

It matters not what your family, friends, community or your colleagues accept you or not. It is what you do with your disability is what will count.

As you work with your disabled population, you are getting a glimpse of what you will be facing. Some of you will not be able to cope with your new disability because of what you experience here.

Some of you will commit suicide rather than face the new disability.

Others of you will embrace the new challenge and show the world what you can accomplish but knowing inside you it is just a show.

However, most of you will realize it is a matter of practicality and time.

For whatever the reason, you'll go on doing what you need to do until you die, more afraid of death than the disability you acquired."

Again, I was hoping to see some expression on their faces, but the scene did not change. I was not sure if the translator was conveying my thoughts correctly or not.

I then cross-examine the young lady in the back asking for her opinion of what I said.

She seemed quite a surprise that I would ask her.

She glanced to see the Director towards the front her to get a nod from her boss that she could speak. He nodded yes.

She said in broken English she never thought about it, other than that, she knew she would be old someday. Then she said the same thing in Russian. The staffs all turn their heads toward her as she went on.

Still seeking approval from her boss, she started to tell me as she interpreted to her colleagues her thoughts about becoming disabled person in the future.

Mostly it was about her hoping that she would not be like that patients in this hospital. She felt there was not much hope for these patients and there would not be any hope for her.

I then asked her if she could ask the rest of staff if they felt the same way. My interpreter gave me the look has to say, "What am I here for?" for not asking her to interpret.

It was a long pause, and then she said something to them, I not understand but each, one by one state their position or opinion about becoming a disabled person.

Many had thought about it but put it in the back of their mind as to say, "I will wait until then . . ." attitude!"

"I do not know if I have new answers for you or if you will teach me new things that I do not know".

Still I was not getting the response I wanted from them. Nevertheless, they seemed to be a lot more conservation going between them.

Just that, I did not know if the conversation were about the subject at hand or if my presentation they were being critique.

I tried hard to think of a joke or something good to end on my presentation.

My mind race through all my past jokes and witty comments, but nothing came to mind.

Then I blurred out loudly, "I hoped they have cognac to warm up my hooks when I came to see them."

Even my interpreter laughed as she translated my comment. That seems to break the ice a little.

CHAPTER 13
P. R. Campaign

Internats

The following days for one whole week, my entourage of my interpreter, my old hag care giver, our driver and I spent touring other hospitals in the region, "Psycho-neurological internats", or just "internats" as they call them.

I am going to quote a paper on internats I found on the internet that very well explained what we see on the tour but also the state of the Internats system in Russia. Here are selected excerpts.

Violence and children with disabilities:—an international perspective

In russia in the 1990's, children were abandoned to the state at a rate of more than 100,000 per year.

At age four, these and other children who are labeled retarded or "oligophrenic" ("small-brained") were sent to locked and isolated "psycho-neurological internats." according to one russian doctor, these internats were "like a prison to the brain. There's a total lack of sensory stimulation.

We found in a 1998 investigation that russian babies who were classified as disabled were segregated into separate rooms where they were changed and fed, but were bereft of stimulation and lacking in medical care. Confined to cribs, they stared at the ceiling and were not encouraged to walk or talk.

At least 30,000 children at the time of our inquiry had been labeled "ineducable," and relegated to the psycho-neurological internats, where many were confined to cots, often on bare rubber mattresses, and left to lie half-naked in their own urine and feces. Children deemed "too active" or "too difficult" were often placed in dark and barren rooms, sometimes tethered to a bench or their bed by a limb. Others were restrained in makeshift straightjackets made of dingy cotton sacks pulled over the torso and drawn at the waist and neck.

Pasted from <http://www.riglobal.org/publications2/10_24.htm>

Mdir Publication Observations

Medical-pedagogical commissions emphasize to family members that they could never provide the care and education that the child requires to succeed.

Children who are placed in the ministry of labor and social development internats at the age of four face a different situation. Generally speaking, these children are deemed "uneducable.

While there appears to be varying levels of agreement with medical-pedagogical commissions on the part of parents, professionals who make up these commissions clearly believe that they know what is best for these children and that state facilities can meet these children's special needs far better than their parents. In a sense, they are realistic, acknowledging the parents' need to work outside the home and their lack of time available to devote to a child with special needs. In another sense, there is a clear imbalance of information and power. Parents do not fully understand their child's needs and lack the training to address them; therefore, the medical-pedagogical commission single-handedly decides a child's fate in many cases. Parents are frequently said to have "abandoned" their children when, in fact, they were never offered the supportive services necessary to keep them at home.

For children deemed so disabled that they need to be placed in a residential institution, residential institutions are under the authority of the Ministry of Education and Ministry Of Labor and Social Development

---

Boys and girls have separate sleeping quarters with bedrooms containing eight to twenty beds each. Children are generally divided according to their diagnosis or level of ability. In some internats, however, we observed a family-style living arrangement where children of mixed ages lived in one section of the internat as a "family." the furnishings of the internats vary from one site to the next, but they generally have some decorations, sufficient bedding and linens, and recreation rooms. In almost every internat we visited, there is a lack of personal space and a place to keep personal belongings.

Pasted from <http://www.mdri.org/mdri-web-2007/ publications/russia3.html>

Most Internats houses we seen were much smaller than our hospital. Many of the smaller Internats were between 150 and 200 children in the age range of 5 to 18 years old. In Moscow was the larger Internats we visited were between 500 to 600 residents.

Each the administers were inform of our coming, they seem to understand that I going to promote their Internats and help raise money to improve their facilities, get much need medical equipment, upgrading staff training and raise the salary of employees.

I hope to use the latter as a carrot stick to take better care of these children with what resources they already had in their hand.

Getting Control of Internat Abuses

The administrators of hospital all said about the same thing, that they read the same type of reports above. They insisted they were doing the best they could with what resources they were getting.

When I brought the question of child abuses we had seen on our trip, some said it because they hard pressed to find anybody to work with these children for the salary they were getting, but are trying to deal with the problem as best they can with the people they had to hire.

I told them we could come with a good P. R. Campaign but the abuses would cost P. R. Campaign dearly. "We need to get the abuses under control, now!" I added.

Community Help

I suggested that administrator go out to their communities and ask for their corporation on the premise that their assistance would bring much needed money to the community where employees lived.

The images of the community helping the Internats would go a long way to help raise monies.

They said they understood and would implement newer policies dealing with abuse immediately.

Some said they already started community involvement and other said they would start getting community involvement going very soon.

There were lots of "Yes's" comings from these administrators. But I also think they were under orders to act on my P.R. recommendations or lose their jobs.

CHAPTER 14

The brainteasers

Tillamook Cheese

While sitting in foyer with my laptop in front of warm fireplace, the English-speaking staff member from the administrative meeting came down from her room to warm herself at the common fireplace, not knowing I was going to be there.

As she entered the room, she was surprise to see me and then started to turn around to return to her room.

I stood up asking if she join me for some for some hot chocolate and Tillamook Medium Cheddar Cheese loaf, which I brought with me from the U.S., which I cut up with my old trusty cheese cuter in my room with my feet and brought it down to the foyer to snack on while on my computer. However, I did not inform her how I cut the cheese.

At first she acted as she was disrupting me, I said no she was not. I of course add a little guilt by saying it would not be diplomatic to turn me down. She smiled, nodded her head yes and thank me for the invitation.

I thanked her answering my question during the administrative staff meeting to enabling to speak directly to a staff member without an interpreter as she sat in an old rocking chair next to me as I first offered her to serve herself to a cup of some of my hot chocolate from a metal pitcher the house staff had prepared for me, while mine was already served in a glass full of ice. I was waiting for it to cool down.

She poured herself a cup, then I had to twist her arm to taste the Tillamook Cheese.

She partakes by first smelling the aroma, then taking a small bite and then stuff a small piece into her mouth. She said it was good but not strong as the cheeses in Russia and said she would pick some cheese for me to try the next time she goes to the nearby village.

She picked some more pieces of cheese with some crackers then poured herself another cup of hot chocolate and sat back on the rocker. She said she had a long day and looked relieved that she could sit down and rest.

I asked her how day went.

She replied that it was a long day her as she prepared lots patients to the medical ward. I did know she was referring to Building 5, where I have not seen not seen any patients in the operating rooms or if she it was one referring one of the wards that they considered a medical ward.

I did not pressure her for her to clarify her statement, as she looked she had enough questions thrown at her work.

Busted My Bubble

We exchanged lots of pleasantry as we got to know each other.

She soon busted my bubble that maybe I could score with her that evening or soon.

She said that her boy friend was station at the air base next to the hospital complex and flew a number of missions for the hospital.

Thinking he was bringing medicines that were need for the hospital. Then she said, something, which peak my interest. She added that he helped save many lives all over Russia by transporting transplant organs form children who died here at the hospital.

Pressing her for more details, like how did they have the body parts donated and where were they flown to. She simply said from here and to anywhere they needed. She then excused herself saying that, she was tried, and needs to get ready for bed.

I did not think she was covering up anything, but it was a new aspect of what some of services, the hospital provided and would add some good P. R. material for the hospital image, I thought.

I said good night to her as my ego was deflated. She picked up more cracker and cheese as she rose and put down her empty cup on table and bided me a good night.

I turn to my laptop to make some notes of our conversation and adding them to my One Notes program files.

CHAPTER 15

Seeing Blue Eyed Blinker

Each time I came to Building 4, I always made a pilgrim stop to see the Blinker (Blue Eyes).

He always had a different series of blinks that he wanted me to learn as I came each time. I am sure it was a code, he wanted me to learn from him.

My interpreter seemed bored each time we came until I ask him to add various combinations of numbers through the interpreter. He adding them up in his head then spelled each of the results total by blinking each number as my interpreter wrote them down.

Seeing the correct results from her paper, the interpreter, started to get interest in the young boy abilities.

New Ways to Communicate

One time I made eyes gestures to Blinker about my interpreter as if I was saying how good looking she was. With his eyebrows, he showed he agreed. Now we had eyebrows to our means of communications and the interpreter who now wanted to help in a quest to find a way to communicate with his resources.

In my office and dinner, my interpreter and I got into many storm brain sessions, where we discussed all the possibilities of using electronic devices to capitalize on his eyes and eyebrows movements.

We thought about an eye-tracking device used in the military, where pilots and soldiers pointed with just their eyes at target and shoot at it. A laser light could to point to a talk board or move a cursor using an On-Screen Keyboard within the monitor to type out words.

We were going to write for grant to get equipment and private teacher for our Blinker.

As time elapsed, I would go visiting him more often as I did noticing more cues, more eye games, but our languages keep us from really communicating.

We would take him for little rides in the limo, first around the hospital, his nurses would complained we were messing up their routines with him gone.

The limo driver knew we were getting in trouble with the nurse and apparently planned to coordinate the time where we went with Blinker.

As more time and trust we had with the nurses, they even would have Blinker special food go with us when we went beyond Blinker lunch time at the hospital.

I once caught the limo driver and Blinker playing with their eyes, seeing who would blink first. I sure the driver grew fond of Blinker too.

Blinker seemed to enjoy going out with us on these short trip out of the hospital. On several occasions, as we passed the air base, he now associated what vibrations his felt everyday from his bed in the hospital as jets were taking off with the images of the jets he saw from the car that vibrated him as they were taking off.

We all felt frustrated that we could not communicate better or understand what was going on in his head with him.

Even thou he could not seem to be able to smile, his blue eyes flickering excitably as he seen things he liked, specially the jets because I think he could feel them vibrate.

He seemed to understand what we said to him, but it frustrated him when we could not understand him while he wanted to communicate or tell us his wants.

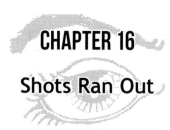

CHAPTER 16

Shots Ran Out

The Shooting

As we were talking in my office about what we could do for Blinker, two loud shots ran out from the outside our building. We heard people yelling, we both run to the window to see what was going on.

As we looked down to the courtyard, we could see a man in heavy winter clothes wave a large pistol as hospital personnel took cover.

We could see a nurse down on the snow who apparently shot and seen the blood from her body spreading on the snow below her.

He was shouting loudly and giving commands, but I did not understand what he was saying. My interpreter said it was something about his son. I could see there was no one could get to the nurse who lay helpless in front of the gunman. Then the interpreter looking out said it the Nurse Lendroma.

I thought to myself maybe her husband? But then I remember, it could not be her husband; he died in the car accident.

Getting Involved

"I am going down, you stay here!" I ordered my interpreter. Then ran down the stairs fast as I could, passing staff members who were very frighten by the shooting.

I got to the door and opened and shouting to the man in English, trying to get his attention. "Sir, I am coming out, I am Gilbert Frederick, a staff member here." As he turn and pointed the gun in my direction.

My interpreter was standing behind me started to shout to him, what I just said.

"I told you to stay upstairs!" I told her in a whisper.

"And who going interpret what you say, John Wayne?" She whispered back.

"Ok, but you stay here! . . . Help me take my shirt and arms off!" I commanded her again.

"What are you going to do?" Again whispering but stronger, as she looked right at my face, as the man still shouting in the background.

"He will see I am unarmed!" I told her.

She strongly said more loudly in a whisper voice. "This is not a joke, this man will kill you!"

"We'll see? Stay here!" I said as my arms came off my shoulder onto her arms and then had her pull my t-shirt off, that I use as a stump sock between my body and artificial limbs.

Facing the Gunman

I put my head out to show him my face, then slowly came out showing him I was truly unarmed by turning my body all way around.

I didn't know if it was my English or not wearing any arms that really got is attention.

He pointed his gun right at me, as he gave me instruction to come toward him.

I again said "I am Gilbert Frederick, a staff member here"

Then a nervous voice right behind me was interpreting my words. As I looked back, her arms were up in the air with her blouse open and flying in the light cold breeze, with no bra, showing she too was unarmed as she made a 360 degree turn for him.

As she finish turning, I gave her a sterner aspirated look, as if I was saying "What are you doing here?", then she whisper back saying. "Where you go, I go!", Then she added "It is my job!"

"I came to ask you if I could see the nurse on the ground, she a friend of mine" I said to him as I waited for the interpretation.

Then I turn my face looking at his gun pointing inches from my forehead until she finish interpreting my last words. I think she added more words than I said.

He then looked at the interpreter listening to her words, then saying towards her direction.

Seeing His Boy

"She would not let me see my boy!"

As his words were coming out, I realized that he has been drinking heavily. I did not need an interpretation; I could smell the odor of heavy liquor from his breath as he was talking.

"Please sir, let me look at her.!" I pleaded again with him.

He looked into my eyes and then my missing arms, saying in a heavy Russian voice. "She would not let me see my boy!" She finished interpreting to me from him.

"No sir, she was protect her own son, who a patient in there." Pointing with my nose and said again to make it clearly to him. "She just was protecting him, Sir!"

As my interpreter finished, his head dropped as he realize why she had stopped him.

He then motioned me, to see her.

Rescuing the Nurse

As I came upon her, I could hear her faint breathing, as her lungs took in short breaths. Her eyes engaged mine as I bend to talk to her and look at her wounds. She said word in Russian, words that I could not make out. Later I learn, she was saying, "Take care of my children, they need each other."

I asked him for his coat, he took it off annoyingly transferring the pistol from one hand to another, as he took off his coat.

As the interpreter took it, she moved close to Nurse Lendorma body and place the coat as I instructed her.

I rolled her with my knees on to the coat, taking a closer look at her wounds. She been shot in the right arm, and a wound near had a punctured wound just above her right breast, it was bleeding profusely.

I, then told the interpreter to take her blouse off, then rolled it and press hard on that wound, to slow down the bleeding, as she covered Nurse Lendroma, then she closed the coat tightly over her body.

I ask him, if she, could be taken by the staff, while I waited with him and talk with him.

After listening to my interpreter's words, he nodded yes. I think he was becoming more sober.

I then told my interpreter to yell to the staffers to bring a gurney or stretcher to us with only two males, I added.

They already seemed prepared as one male and one nurse, the "Cold Nurse" came running out of the building with a gurney in tow behind them.

As they approached us, the "Cold Nurse" began shouting at him. "Почему ты застрелить ее?." Again, later on, I was told she was saying. "Why, did you shoot her?. You, stupid man" I then stood between "Cold Nurse" and the man with the gun, not knowing what she said making a face to shut her up. She did as the three of them helped put Nurse Lendorma on the gurney, even the gunman helped, clutching his pistol under his left armpit.

As they pulled away, the "Cold Nurse" gave the gunman another very dirty look. You could see the "Cold Nurse" was very concern for Nurse Lendorma, as a tear came falling of her face.

As they neared the building, some nurses and doctors rush the gurney to help bring Nurse Lendorma into the building as a doctor opened the coat to see the wounds. They disappeared into the building to treat her.

His Story

It was very cold, as my interpreter and I turned to the man, shivering as we talked to him.

He then began telling up what had happen.

The internat man (The Ministry of Labor and Social Development) told him that it would be better for his son to be in the Internats system. He said he refused. The internat man they would be given stipends for his family to come and visit his son. However, it was not enough to be taking any public transportation here.

He said the used the stipend for the other children school and food during the famine.

He said he wrote the hospital (**Ministry of Labor and Social Development**) many times, but told nothing.

He ran into the "internat man" on the streets of his hometown, warning him if he does not tell him where his son is, he would shoot him.

Using me as the "internat" man, he pointed his gun to my head. Just then that I forgot how cold I was getting.

He was talking to my interpreter, then, glancing, once in awhile, toward me as he used his gun to make his points.

I was worried the gun might go off, I asked him if we could have the gun.

Looking as he lost all hope, he said he would if he could see his son. I promised we would look for his son together, but not with a gun in his hand.

With a little more prompting from the interpreter, he nodded yes.

Unarming him, interpreter takes gun, but she seemed nervous hold the gun and shaking from the cold.

Looking For His Son

As we started for the hospital building, as the police and Military Police arrived, pointing guns at us from a distance. Them not knowing who was who, they ordered us to lay down on the snow. We didn't because it was too cold.

You could see the young soldiers looking at my interpreter's bare breasts, which she was try to keeping them warm by wrapping her arms over them, while holding the pistol. Others were looking at my bear upper body with missing arms. Some were looking at both, wondering which body they should focus on. Maybe she won, she had the gun!

I told an officer, who seemed to be in charge who I was, then shouting at him I said "He came to see his son and he will, I promised him for the gun."

As my interpreter was interpreting, she held the gun as if, we meant business. You know that "John Wayne" looks.

The officer objected, and then said only if we take an escort and give the soldier the gun.

I said "No". Then proceed to go into the hospital with the father in front of us with our cold bear back to officer as my interpreter was saying. "We be, right back!"

There was nothing they could do, there were too many staffers in front of us. They could not shoot us without hit one or more of them.

They stood there like a SWAT standoff, trying to get the staff to leave the building, but nobody moved as we entered. We had the gun!

Some staffers put a warmed blanket on both our shoulders, as we entered, then they offered one to the father, but he refused.

The blanket felt so very good, I could feel me becoming un-thawed as more warm blankets were placed on us. Even hot coffee and tea, was being offered. The interpreter took the coffee and I took a sip from a cup, being held for me by one of the nurses.

They all seemed to have heard our conversion outdoors on the snow and understanding the gunman story.

While we were walking, I told my interpreter to open the chamber of the pistol to take the bullets out. She was having a hard time with it until one of staffers took it, unloaded it and gave it back to her, but she refused. The staffer held on to it as he followed us.

All this was un-be-knowing to the police and soldiers outside.

The gunman, now just a father, told us that a staffer had told him, because son age, he would be in Building 4.

Unknown to us, the "Cold Nurse" was blocking the entrance to the building to the police and soldiers, with her staff locking the door behind us.

We walked from bed to bed, ward to ward, floor to floor and then, looking at a seas of beds, he instantly saw his son, three rolls back as we entered almost the last ward.

His son had a tube running out of his nose. He rushed to him, as he made it to the opposite side of the bed avoiding a handcart type cart on wheels holding a tall slender oxygen tank. Gazing at his son, he put his hand on his head, then started crying, as big wet tears started rolling down his weather worn face

I don't know what he was saying, but all of us and the ward staffers were quite, it even seemed the other children were silent in that ward.

There was no sound or eye contact nor an expression on his son face, as the father bend down to look at him. The father's tears still streaming down from his face as he looked at the oxygen tank, grasping the his son's tube, then he fixed his eyes on his son.

It seemed like an hour went by, but was only minutes before the father stood upright. Again, he said something to his son and kissed him. I think he realized his son needed the hospital.

As we walked out and into the hall, he really looked resigned as if he knew what awaited his outside.

As we got to the locked door, we could see an officer and a soldier looking in windows on each side of the doors.

The "Cold Nurse" without changing her dirty look at the father, unlocked the door. After short time standing as the door was unlocked, he surrender to the first soldiers he encountered. The staffer holding the gun gives up the gun to another soldier just outside the door.

CHAPTER 17

It's over!

We never knew what had happen to the father, but I knew what happened to all the staff, we all came together as a hospital organization. Nothing was said, but everyone there felt like a hero of sorts as we all congratulated each other.

I am sure as the other hospital units in the complex heard what had happen, there was some type of unity happening among them.

Many were smiling at me for the first time. I did not get one from the "The Cold Nurse" but never the less I felt it from her as she approached us and told us where Nurse Lendorma was taken to.

"Come on John Wayne" let get you armed and see how Nurse Lendorma is doing." Said my interpreter as if she said like a cowgirl would say it. She hugged me, as she put her arms holding her blanket around me, I could feel her bear breast, still cold upon my bear chest.

After getting my arms, the police escorted us while asking us a lot of questions. We were careful as we made our remarks supporting the father actions and excusing him because he was really intoxicated.

Check On Nurse Lendorma

With my unbutton shirt just hanging loosely around my upper body, we walked over to the medical building where they took Nurse Lendorma for emergency treatment.

The Cold Nurse lead us saying she would be all right, they were waiting for an ambulance to take her to a air base hospital next door.

As we came nearer to Nurse Lendroma emergency bed, she tried smiling at us but you could tell she still was in pain, even though they gave her pain medications.

The Doctor at her side said they were able to stop the bleeding but needed x-rays to see if they were any internal damages.

I could see at the end of the bed that the "Cold Nurse" had place her hands on Nurse Lendorma foot to reassure her that should be Ok!

I told Nurse Lendorma through, my interpreter, that the man been arrested but he did get to see his son, without the gun.

This sparked words rushing out her mouth saying, someone needed to go see her daughter and explain to her what has happen. The interpreter assured we would go to see her daughter without me saying it.

Her Daughter

Tears were starting to flow as we talk to her about her daughter. Still not telling me what was going on between her son and daughter. An ambulance crew just entered before I could question her more. As they prepared her for transportation all I could make out of her trying to talk to us. "My daughter! My daughter! Please, take care of her!" Again, without me saying anything, my interpreter told her we would.

I remember her words her said about her daughter before, again she repeated say the same thing over and over as she went down the hall and into the ambulance.

I knew a little bit of Russian by now, to partly understand what my interpreter was saying to her as she accompanied Nurse Lendorma to the ambulance.

As we seen her off, the Hospital limo came up in place where the ambulance once stood. Again, the "Cold Nurse" must have had arranged it. "Those Russians could really think ahead." I said to myself.

Nurse Lendorma's Daughter

In the limo, my interpreter button my shirt and tried to tuck it inside my pants, but since we were sitting it was kind of hard for her as I lifted my ass from the seat with my neck pushing on the my headrest.

The limo driver knew exactly where we were going. He drove right to Nurse Lendorma home or really it was series of small apartments, each about four stories high. Nurse Lendorma's apartment was on the second floor.

We knocked at Nurse Lendorma's apartment, an old lady, who watches Nurse Lendorma daughter during day, open the door. She had a very concern face as she already heard the news about Nurse Lendorma.

She said, "Are you the American at the Hospital?" in broken English, I started to say yes, but my interpreter was more concern about the daughter and cut me off.

My interpreter took charged of the situation as I felt I lost all control of her. She asked many questions of the old lady and then moved on to the bedroom, where the daughter was as I followed her in.

She had been crying, but stopped as we came in. The daughter first gazed at my limbs as she already heard about me, now being I confirm what her mother said about me.

She seemed to look very sickly to me.

Again, my interpreter asked the old lady about what was wrong with the child as I observed the daughter reaction to what the old lady was saying about her.

I asked my interpreter what was being said, because the daughter was had said some words to my interpreter as the old lady was talking to her. My interpreter said the daughter was saying that she was not sick, but just tried, as the old lady saying how sick she was.

Then my interpreter turned her attention to the little girl. Apparently, after talking to her about her mother being at the hospital, the little girl demand to see her mother. My interpreter assuring her that the mother was going to be all right. She picked up the little girl and said to me. "We are going to take her to the hospital to see her mother. Now go tell the limo driver where we are going." She ordered.

As I was going down the stair, it came to me that my interpreter would make a good mother. Then it occurred to me, how am, I going to tell the driver where we are going.

As I approached the limo, the limo driver, quickly got out from his seat, came to open my side of the door. I said in English, in a short sentence and deliberately slower. "We go to Nurse Lendorma hospital." He nodded yes, as if he already knew where we were going.

"Do these Russian, wear ear pieces or what?" I said to myself in amazement. Like, as he could read my mind; then he was nodded "No!", as it seem he was answering me.

Standing outside the limo waiting for the daughter and my interpreter, the limo driver reached inside my side of the door, pulled out my overcoat and placed on my shoulders.

As they came out, the old lady was putting on her coat. She was coming along with us.

The old lady was smiling in amazement as she looked at the limo. As we entered, the old lady stopped to wipe her feet on a stone laying next to the limo.

Both the daughter and the old lady took a long look at their surrounding in the limo.

I started talking to my interpreter in English, asking what was going on? Apparently, the little girl had walk out of the apartment and was caught by the old lady on the street, saying she was going to see her mother at the hospital, but heading in the wrong direction before we arrived. This was the reason she was crying when we came to her bedroom.

The interpreter said, when she asked about the family financial situation, the old lady told that there was little food in apartment and was very cold at night, because the steam heaters in the apartments were closed after 11 PM each night to conserve on the coals, which feed the boiler. The old lady also told her that she stay with them without pay, just to have a place to live. She was homeless when Nurse Lendorma founder on the street.

We decided before we got to the hospital, that they would stay in my bedroom and I would sleep on the sofa. My place was much bigger than my interpreter. It was getting late to arrange any help for them.

The hospital visit was short, because her Nurse Lendorma had just came out of surgery to repair a hole on the upper part of her right lung pieced by the bullet from gunman pistol. She was still coming out of sedation but sleeping comfortably in her hospital bed.

As we drove from the hospital, my interpreter was holding the sleeping little girl, with her chin upon the girl head and her eyes closed as if she was sleeping too.

As I watched them both, I wished that I had a family, but I screwed things up twice when I had the chance to keep a family. Then I wished that I could be with my interpreter in her bed tonight, for now I wanted to be held too.

The next day, it seemed that the word got around about Nurse Lendorma's living conditions and knowing she would not get paid if she was not working, even in this situation.

As we got to the limo, the limo driver and the "Cold Nurse" were packing donated goods and food into the back of the limo. A big pickle jar filled with rubles and coins sat outside the door as personnel had come by to help Nurse Lendorma and her family.

The old lady just could not stop thanking everyone around the limo and those on the sidewalk waiting to see the little girl.

The director's wife gave her a china doll, which she seem to like very much and played with the dolly all the way to her home.

CHAPTER 18

The Inquiring

Then one day while going to see Blinker, I find he is not on the ward.

The Nurse tells me he was move to an older ward because of his age. But no one at that ward knew anything of the boy.

I spent a few hours looking for him.

The Cold Nurse said that these cases sometime get lost because the children do not have ID bracelets or tags on their beds. However, she said eventually their found and put in the right place. She said she knew one that was missing for weeks. Remember, she said there were many children here. Wherever he might be, he will be taking care of real well.

I accepted it for a while but my efforts to find him were to no avail.

I resumed looking for him after work, I did not want another other Derrick, thinking I have abandoned him too.

I even tried putting notice everywhere I could around the hospital complex. I just felt some body knew had to know.

It became almost an obsession with me and my interpreter. The more we tried the colder the staff became, including the limo driver.

It was begins to feel like everybody knew what had happened to him, except me and my interpreter.

A Clue

Sometime later the girl who has a pilot boyfriend, said to me in passing that my Blinker was flown to Moscow by her boyfriend, but she did not want to elaborate.

I tried several times to catch her at work or at the residence. I did not succeed.

I talk to the Director, but he said that I needed more information on the boy, a case number or his name. All of which we never thought of getting when we had contact with him. We just call him Blinker, he seem to like that name.

We had the director ask for list of all patients transfer out of that building during the disappearance of Blinker.

The list covered the whole month, with nearly 40 names on it, 22 to the medical ward and the rest to Building 4. We had ready talk to Building 4 personnel but could not tell us what had happened to Blinker. They claimed they did not know him before the transfer and thereby could not help ID him. They said, all the patients are all were known by their case numbers only. Nobody paid attention to how they looked; they were all nameless children, who just needed to be monitor by just their numbers.

There were no photos to go by, just a face in the interpreter and my memories.

No one had paid any attention to the time we were with Blinker; they consider our time with him as a waste of our time.

We followed up on the 22 children that went to the medical ward, but they too said they did not have him there, just saying that they often died there because of some illness they had. Without a number, they could not help us.

Later when I heard that he might have been flown to Moscow, I went back to the medical ward.

They said they only send cadavers or the very sick to the Medical school so med students could practice on them.

That was not in itself that unusual in the states for people in the know, we call them County Hospital, where our poor terminal ill Americans and the illegal's go and become guinea pigs.

However, without a number or name they could not tell us what had happen to Blinker, but provided information by the Id number who died or was transfer to the medical school hospital.

They add that the children who were sick usually all died there from complications or a bad student treatment.

We were at a dead end; all we got was a promise that they would do a better job of keeping track of them and testing these children.

CHAPTER 19
The Interpreter

Natasha

I found out my interpreter first name was Natasha, I realized I always referred to her as "My interpreter!"

Up to now, she was cold; would spend the whole day with me as well at dinner table. After dinner, having enough of me, she would go to her room and not come out until she would me for breakfast and start our day together.

Sundays was the only day I did not see her at anytime. I do not know if she stayed her room or left the hospital grounds. Her private life was just that, <u>Private</u>!

Blinker Broke the Ice

She too wanted to know what happen to Blinker. I believe she wanted to find him as bad as I did.

Natasha asked me why was Blinker so important to me?

"Because that boy could of have been me. Wanting to be heard, to be loved, and care for. Being different is so very lonely." I said to her and then added. "I know loneliness so well, so very well!"

I told her that many people like me were put in state hospitals in forties and early sixties without a hearing, just on recommendations of a doctor in the U.S . . .

Some of state hospitals were almost as bad as the Internats or Russian State Hospitals that we both had visited. The State of California had tried putting my sister and me into Fairview State Hospital at one point. My sister Josephine, four years younger than me, had encephalitis and polio.

Going to Moscow

As I was making plans to go to Moscow. I asked Natasha to in to my office. I asked her to arrange for an interpreter and an attendant and to meet me at the Air Hotel in Moscow the following week.

She replied that she was assign to me by the government, not the hospital. Where I went, she went! As, if I should of known, that!

So, then I said "I still need an attendant. She said, "I'll take care of that too!" I did not really know what that meant.

Is she volunteering to undress and bathe me?

I asked her if nudity would brother her.

Nudist

"No!" She said she is a nudist.

I laughed, then had her take out my membership card to AANR, (American Association for Nude Recreation) from my purse-wallet and showed to her.

She laughed after reading it.

"Show me yours!" I insisted.

"I can prove you I am a nudist! I have photos of me naked." She said as she went next door to her office, came back and pullout a small photo album book from her purse.

Anticipating I was going to see an adult woman naked, it was a photo of a nudist wedding with three nude breasts-less teen-age girls holding a train of the nude bride and asked. "Which one are you? These girls are pre-teens, right?"

"No, I was thirteen at the time, I am the tall slider one with braids . . . I just starting to develop, late! Those are my sisters, we were the bride's maids, that is my mother, my oldest brother and his bride" She said as she described the people in the photo and pointing each of them out.

"Your whole family, are nudists? I queried her.

"Yes! My parents were nudists before I was born." She responded.

"My family thinks I am a devil in the nude! I retorted.

She smiled as she seem to understand the other option of others about nudity, she continued saying. "My grandfather was one of the founders of the St. Petersburg Free Body Cultural Society. He refers often to the Rosiches or Rus, the medieval mix of Slavs and Vikings who gave Russia her name.

> *"When perun was impregnating the earth with bolts of lightning during violent storms . . . of Rus, ' . . . the ancient Russians would strip naked and roll in the wet grass with their horses and cattle in the belief that they would all, humans and animals alike, thus acquire some of nature's potent vitality".*

"*The Russian Bath . . .*" My grandfather would explain. " . . . is a time-honored "living example" of the Rodiche passion for cleanliness and natural living."

> *The baths were communal for everyone including children, though washing rooms have always been segregated by sex.*
>
> *The steam and dressing rooms were also communal.*
>
> *The Peasant tone of Russian life was very close to nature, and nudity was understood to be a part of it, a simple, social style of behavior."*

She seem like she was quoting her grandfather.

Summer Solstice

I felt as she was going to lecture on the virtues of Russian nudism, as I think she often does as if I was a tourist on a tour.

> *"The evening of Ivana-Kupala celebrates our Summer Solstice, June 21-22, the shortest night of the year. It is like your,*

Halloween and Easter in the United States, it is a celebration that is deeply rooted in our pagan history.

The ancient Rus origins of this festivity revolved around fertility and self purification, the idea being clean one's body, mind and spirit in order to gain an elevated consciousness.

The pagan roots of the celebration promoted fertility, and echoes of this resonate today in an event known for its often ribald [humorous but rude and vulgar, often involving jokes about sex] ebullience [full of cheerful excitement or enthusiasm]).

The Eve of Ivana-Kupala was a "Night of Love" when married couples were released from the usual strictures governing daily life.

On this night it was accepted if a husband chose another woman or girl from among his wife's friends or family.

Similarly, it was acceptable should a wife select a male partner from her husband's friends and family.

On the day following Kupala's Eve, it was also believed that certain grasses and plants acquired supernatural qualities,

In the morning the young people went out to the fields to collect Kupalenka, medvez'ye ushko (little bear ears), bogatenka (the grass of the reach men) and razryv-trawa (love-break-grass) which were then placed at the head of the bed to encouraging dreams, which on this night were considered to be prophetic". She finishes in a romantic tone.

As she was talking, all I could think about was her holding my penis as she would be washing it on our upcoming trip to Moscow.

"What are you thinking about?" She asked me as she notices I was not completely listening to her.

"Oh, just about what you were saying." I quickly responded.

"You males, as it seems to me, visit the clothes-optional beach to show them off and to look at the young and pretty women.

Naturism gives men a chance to show their power, charm and their other characteristics-like a peacock does!—and I think this behavior has a root in ancient primordial human marriage rituals." She lectured me again.

"I think your right!" Saying this, I was thinking of my "love addition". How many members does your group have?
"Our particular group set the limit at 500 official members.

But, because we are an open Society and we say welcome to all who would like to spend his/her time with us, there are in fact many more.

For example, on a hot Sunday gathering, with games and competitions on the beach, we usually have more than 5,000-6,000 guests." She informs me.
"How has your group been received by the new government in Russia?" I asked her as if I was interviewing her.
"Without any problems!" She asserted.

"The government would much prefer to see groups such as ours instead of porno-studios and porno-cinemas.

There are many printers in Russia producing terrible and tasteless pornography, so groups such as ours are a welcome way for society to deal with nudity.

What kind of people join Naturist groups such as yours?

It remains today that, as a rule, the average Russian naturist represents the middle to lower economic classes of Russians.

Representatives of the "New Russian Reach People" (major businessmen), presently prefer not to relax on a clothing-optional beach that is open to the public.

The social mask of big businessmen imitated the lifestyle of the prosperous Western nouveau riche, including (from the nouveau riche viewpoint) a few compulsory elements":

Vacation only on the most fashionable beaches of the West

Follow the Western fashion of snow-white skin among the Upper Class

A belief that sunburn and intense solar radiation is harmful.

Is it legal to be nude in public in Russia? I questioned again.

"Only in the place where it is reasonable: on the Clothes Optional Beach and in Russian Baths."

Interestingly, none of the official registered Russian societies are referred to as "nudist."

Instead, we have societies named "Healthy Lifestyle," "Society of Sun Fans," "Free Body Culture Society," and various clubs such as "Harmony," "Sun" and "Aqua."

"Why?" begged to know.

"Because "nudism" is not a Russian word" She posed and then she added. "Also, the practice of "nudism" was historically connected with illegal behavior from the point of view of Soviet leaders."

"So your Society is a religion one?" I inquired.

"Well, most of us consider Naturism as a "nonreligious religion." She explained

"Beside your Kupala's Night, what is the most important celebration as a nudist group?" I inquired, hoping that she

would invite me to join her at one. You know, as a follow nudist of course!.

"Of course the other important events are: The start of Summer Naturist season (on Easter), Children's Day (June 1), Independence Day of Russia (June 12) Birthday of Naturist Csar Cyrill the First (June 25) and The End of Naturist Summer (First Saturday of November)!"

"Isn't it too cold to run around naked then?" I stuttered pretending to tremble.

There are brave and crazy Russian nudists that weather the sub zero temperatures of large bodies of water in Russia in the heart of the coldest of winters. Hypothermia or not, they believe so strongly in naturism that they risk their bodies in freezing waters and icy conditions, like naked polar bears, to experience nature at its most brutal. If that isn't a true exhibition of a desire to experience nature, then I certainly don't know what is.

There are nudist and naturist organizations all over the country from border to border, and in all the major cities including even Moscow. There are even Russian nudist organizations in the heart of the most god awful inhabited land, perhaps, on the face of this planet. Russian naturists even exist in what was once a winter prison known as Siberia.

"I was glad it was not snowing in Moscow." I said to myself, thinking she would drag me into snow in the nude for me to show her how manly I was.

Bear It All

We arrived late in the afternoon, at dinner; we got to know a little more about each other.

She said she was still single, her job was too demanding and needed to travel a lot to get married. Her parents were still alive and healthy. When she visits her hometown, in St. Petersburg where she would go out with her brother and already young adults sister and hit the street of night parties and movies.

We were share a double room suite with a common living room, which includes a fireplace, at Air Hotel, 500 meters up the main road from the airport.

Like most nudists after enter the room we shed our clothes, she helped me undress and then she got undressed. She then offered to bath me in the shower. The shower was large for 2-4 people, so I motioned to join me and she did.

She had a very beautiful body, small breast and a tight ass. It was all could do from keeping my penis from erecting.

She dried us off and return to the main room where a fireplace was already going. She sad on a fur mat on the floor and I sat on a footstool next to her.

We gaze at the ambers flying around in the fireplace. Both us were relaxing in presence of one another.

She was not the cold interpreter that I knew all the time we been together, she was a very warm, seemly lonely women. She was not the stuff-shirt women whom I got to know for past several years.

We talked about nudism in each of our country and then we talked about sexuality in her country. She already knew about sexuality in America, she seemed to have explored sex on the internet. She explained. "On the internet, you Americans can see everything; even see them doing the un-natural."

I responded. "Your Russians contribute a lot to that 'un-natural'.

She returned my charge. "Yes, that the price we pay to compete with your democracy and your way of life."

"You mean all the money your Russians are making on the pono industry in America?" I retorted.

She seems to agree me with a "Yes" nod.

Her Sexuality

I asked about her sexuality, fearing that she was going turn off on me, but said she was cautious with sex, afraid to losing her job.

She then she laid her hand on my leg next to my penis. She made circle jester on the head of my penis and then got up to the television, pull out a movie she seem to know about and put the disk into the DVD player.

She then returned, sat between legs with her back on my penis. My penis was already enlarging from her nearly touching my penis and my gazing sexually at her sexy body.

As we watching a romantic movie with both Russian and English dialogs with slow developing sex scenes.

She, as a matter of fact like, turn within my legs facing me and kissing me then proceeded kissing my body, down my chest to my penis, she reached my penis as she opened her mouth to let my penis enter it. She seems to know exactly what to do. She rubs my balls and wet my penis with her saliva.

I placed my right foot on her vagina rubbing it as my right toe felt it was near to her G sport. It did not seem to matter to her that I was touching her with feet instead of my hands, if I had any.

As she knew I was getting close to climaxing, she pulls away. She rose with her vagina pressing my face. I played and sucked it with tongue then taking little bites at her lobes protruding outside her vagina. The taste and the aroma from the shower linger in around her vagina until her juice began to flow on to my tongue.

As she came close to climaxing, she pulled away again, this time she had me rise, as she kissed again my upper body, then run her tongue around my neck and then to my shoulders to the site of my amputations. She kissed both the amputated sites saying. "Sorry that the bears did this to you."

Then she was tugging on my penis to lead me into her bedroom.

She had me lay down as she climbed on top, straddled me, then

I enter her; still wet, my penis slid in with her hands helping.

She paced herself so I did not climax until we were real hot and sweating. We both seem to explode into prolong climax.

My penis has an penal implant, though I came my penis was still erected as she milked my cum into her mouth, then clasping her body on to mine, pressing her breasts onto my mouth, as I sucked her nipples which were still hard. Her body was flushed and clammy as she slid around my body as to merge both our sweat body into one.

After a half hour or so, she got up and went to the restroom to clean herself, then returned with a hot wet hand towel and proceed to clean my penis as she kissed it as to say good night to it. She then had me rise without a word and pointed me toward my room. I kissed her goodnight as she closed her door behind me.

It has been a long time that I had sex like that. In addition, it was an endless sex play and sexual body contact for the three nights we were together. Each night it ended the same way, as the first without saying any romantic words, just being very sexual satisfied.

CHAPTER 20

The search for Blinker

The daytimes we spent looking for Blinker, went to each hospital and internats, even the morgues of the hospitals and asking staff if they had seen anyone come in from our hospital in a plane. No one remembered just organs or tissues come from there, on a military jet. The one administer of the hospitals said.

For three days, we followed every lead we could think of, but no signs of Blinker turned up.

We return to the hospital with nothing.

As for Natasha, she returns to her work as my interpreter and resume her professionalism, she was cold again as nothing ever happen between us. It was clear to me past few days would never happen again.

I kept thinking there was more I could do to find Blinker. However, I seem to run into a host of blank walls. Something tells me that Blinker disappearance was no accident. Too many things just do not add up.

The girl, who has a boyfriend, pilot, was trying to tell me something; but I cannot pin her down enough to follow up on her comment about possibility of Blinker was flown to Moscow.

Then, they are the records system, with case numbers indexing instead by names.

The file record themselves, a few intake pages and evaluation checklist with the rest being the health, medications, weight logs and growth charts, but no narratives or other case notes or background information are contained in them. When I asked the director, he said coldly, "What is there to say, they are all vegetables!" and ended at that.

Then there is the gloominess of the hospital place and staff.

They way the hospital is organized, a lot of children in the first building and then tapered down to few. Maybe they died off, went to another hospital because they are harder to care for as they grew or into new or a different program in another part of the country. Yet no there is no mention of other facilities or transfers other than the transfers to Moscow.

Then there my observation of the military airport tarmac close to the hospital, the only jet fighters type aircrafts seem to come to that part of the airport. I never even see one that reassembles an air ambulance or small passenger carrying aircraft.

What did see was someone from the hospital handing up to the pilot by a pole, with a package of some sort. Maybe transporting transplant organs form children who died here as she said before at the residence.

At the time, being romantic about it, I thought it was the girl, with the pilot boyfriend, handing him his lunch.

The staff seems to be avoiding me. My questions are aviated, when I ask them directly.

They are better than I am in keeping secrets. They all seemed they have taking a course in "101 Keeping Secrets". Even my interpreter, at times, seems evasive.

Things just did not add-up and all the staff knew my puzzlement, including the director.

CHAPTER 21
The Confrontation

I finally setup an appointment with the director to directly confront him all the information I had on Blinker.

I think he knew what the meeting was going to be all about, Blinker.

I started our meeting by saying that if anyone should know about Blinker was him.

We started to argue about my accusations that something was going on here that is not right, as my interpreter head went back and forth quickly between us as she quickly interpreter our argument went.

He then stopped and pointed me back to a chair in front of his desk, as my interpreter pulled one up for her as he pointed one finger to his lips as to say "To shut up!"

Then slowly, as to give my interpreter a chance to translate every word he was going to say to me.

"This hospital is farm we collect children who are in a vegetated state from all over Russia, Ukraine, Chet Republics and China, with governmental support of those country. These children are just mindless vegetables; they are a burden to their family, to their sociality and to this country. We relieve many family of the burden and financial cost of caring for these children.

They have no mothers or fathers to kiss them good night: their parents abandoned them rather than face the stigma of bringing up an

> "imperfect" child in a society that abhorred disability in Soviet
> times and is little different today".
>
> (The Sunday Times (UK), 'Imperfect' children left to die by Mark
> Franchetti Moscow February 21 1999, [for personal use only])

The thinking parts of the brain of these children are dead!"

"Blinker had a mind! He was not a vegetable he had intelligence! I quickly and loudly inserted.

The director came back with a charge of own, "You did not even bother to know his name, you could have asked him or his nurse to find out his name, no, you just gave him one."

I came back, knowing he was right with, "At least I gave him one, a name! You gave them only case numbers!"

He seemed to acknowledge my point.

He continues about what he was going to say before I interrupted him. "Not one of the members of any of these commissions "On Right of Children", who come here to pass judgments on own county, telling us on how un-trainable children are to be taken care of here in Russia, will not or would not take any of these children their home and personally care for them. As you American say 'Do as I say, not as I do!'"

Here the child is carefully monitor, he or her, health, nutrition and physical care is rigidly maintained."

"So are cows, pigs and zoo animals." I whispered to my interpreter.

"You have a bad habit, Mr. PR man; you like to twist things around. These children live better here than any of the Internats in Russia or in your country.

I know you been to the other internats, or and/or least read about them.

What you know of our facility how do we rate?" he questioned me.

Not stopping he went on. "We have the best nurses, clean facilities, and medicines. Our children do not suffer or are physically abused nor neglected." He said emphatically.

'However, there's a total lack of sensory stimulation and there is no nurturing of these children." I shouted back.

"There is nothing left to nurture." He comments as his voice raise to my sound level.

"However, they are going to die here!" I said very forcibly.

"They were already dead in the internats, when we got them. Their bodies only exist, we are only preserving tissues and organs, so another child lives!

CHAPTER 22

Transplants

"Read this!" Like an lawyer, he handed me a unusual Transplant Timeline list in Russian, my interpreter read it to me from his hand written notes, as if was a research project.

1. *400 BCE to First century CE: First skin grafts/flaps for facial reconstruction: In the work Samhita, Indian author Sushruta describes reconstruction of noses and ear lobes using skin grafts from the cheek. (Early research dates Samhita a from about 600 BCE, but modern historians dispute this date, giving a date of 400 BCE to 1st century CE.)*

2. *1668: Xenotransplant—First successful bone graft: Dutchman Job van Meeneren documents the use of a bone graft from a dog's skull to repair a defect in a human cranium.*

3. *1682: Xenotransplant—Another, or the same bone graft but different date?: A bone from a dog is reportedly used to repair the skull of an injured Russian aristocrat (who is later said to have had the bone removed because of threats of excommunication from the church).*

Meanwhile, jumping to nineteen century there were other claims say . . .

4. *1822: First Skin Transplant (autograft): Berger reportedly performs the first skin autograft—but it can only be the first if the procedure described in Sushruta's Samhita (c. 400 BCE) was theoretical.*

5. *1881: First Temporary Skin Transplant (from a cadaver): A surgeon treats a patient, suffering from burns received while*

leaning against a metal door that was struck by lightning, using skin from a deceased person as a temporary graft.

6. *1906: First Successful Cornea Transplant: Dr. Eduard Zirm, a surgeon working in the Moravian town of Olmutz, performs the first corneal transplant to maintain some degree of transparency. He publishes a paper in the 1906 Archives of Ophthalmology (64:580-591). Few other surgeons match Zirm's success until after the Second World War, when very fine needles and finer silk become available.*

7. *1908: First Knee-joint Transplant: Dr. Erich Lexer of Germany reports performing the first knee-joint transplant (from a cadaver), but the procedure is unsuccessful.*

8. *1911: First Vein Transplant: Dr. Yamanouchi performs the first use of homologous vein tissue in arterial reconstruction.*

9. *1920: Xenotransplant—First Monkey Testicles Transplanted into Human: At his clinic in France, Dr. Serge Voronoff transplants monkey testicles into a man. By the early 1930s, more than 500 men are reported to have received transplanted testicles.*

10. *1964: First Attempted Hand Transplant: A hand is transplanted in Ecuador, but it is rejected within two weeks.*

11. *1969: First Partial Larynx Transplant: A Belgian doctor performs a subtotal transplant of a larynx, but the patient dies without speaking.*

12. *1983: First Multi-Visceral Transplant: The first multi-visceral transplant is performed at the University_of_Pittsburgh_Medical Center in Pennsylvania.*

13. *1985: Ethics: The Ethics Committee of the Council of the Transplantation_Society, an international body, issues guidelines prohibiting the buying and selling of organs and tissues.*

It was this entry that hit me, I realized, that Blinkers eyes might have been sold.

14. *1988: First Sciatic Nerve Transplant: Drs. Alan R. Hudson and Susan E. Mackinnon, of the University_of_Toronto, transplant the sciatic nerve of a 16-year-old female, who died from a hemorrhage, into nine-year-old Matthew Beech, who had his sciatic nerve destroyed in a water-skiing accident. Two years*

after the surgery, Beech could feel pinpricks on the sole of his foot for the first time since the accident, showing that the axons had grown through the graft and down the nerves to the sole of the foot.

15. *1988: First Human Fetal Cell Transplant: University of Colorado doctors implant fetal cells into a patient's brain.*

16. *A follow-up study of Parkinson's patients with transplanted fetal cells, which is published in The_New_England_Journal_of Medicine on November 26, 1992, indicates promising results. However, in a later study, published by several of the same doctors and appearing in the March 8, 2001 NEJM, finds that the cell transplant benefit occurred in younger patients, not older patients, and that 15% of younger patients suffer irreversible side effects known as disabling dyskinesias.*

17. *1998: First Total Larynx Transplant: Dr. Marshall Strome leads a team of Cleveland_Clinic doctors in performing a total larynx transplant on 40-year-old Timothy Heidler, whose larynx was destroyed 20 years before in a motorcycle accident. Three days after the surgery, Heidler is able to speak for the first time since the accident.*

18. *1998: First (Semi) Successful Hand Transplant: Dr. Jean-Michel Dubernard performs a hand transplant on New Zealander Clint Hallam in Lyon, France. After reportedly not following correct anti-rejection treatment or physical therapy, the hand is amputated at the patient's request on February 2, 2001.*

Thou the translation was in English, he seem to be punctuated each entry with his head, sometime add a sound or grunt as my translator read on.

19. *1998: First Unrelated Stem Cell Transplant: Doctors at the AFLAC Cancer_Center_of_Egleston_Children's_Hospital_at_Emory_University in Atlanta perform an unrelated donor cord blood stem transplant on Keone Penn, a 12-year-old with sickle cell anemia. In June 2003, Penn provides testimony about the procedure, which cured his sickle cell disease, before the Senate Commerce, Science and Transportation Subcommittee on Science, Technology and Space.*

20. *2000: First Womb Transplant: Dr. Wafa Fageeh at King Fahad Hospital and Research Centre in Jeddah,_Saudi_Arabia, transplants the uterus of a 46-year-old into a 26-year-old woman. The uterus produces two menstrual periods before it fails after three months and has to be removed.*
21. *2003: First Jawbone Transplant: Surgeons at Rome's Istituto Regina Elena transplant a mandible from the body of a 39-year-old man into an 80-year-old man who has advanced cancer of the mouth.*
22. *2003: First Tongue Transplant: A team of Austrian doctors at Vienna's General Hospital performs a 14-hour tongue transplant on a 42-year-old man suffering from a malignant tumor affecting his tongue and jaw.*
23. *2004: First Ankle Transplant: In August, a team of Italian surgeons led by Dr. Sandro Giannini, transplanted the ankle of a 17-year-old boy (who had died in a car accident) into Silvano Bordon, a 48-year-old rally driver, who had lost mobility of his foot in an accident in 1991.*
24. *2005: First Partial Face Transplant: On November 27, surgeons at a hospital in Amiens in northern France performed the world's first partial face transplant, grafting a nose, lips, and chin onto a 38-year-old woman, Isabelle Dinoire, who had been disfigured by a dog bite received in May 2005.*

My sexuality got a boost as I read the next passage.

25. *2006: First Penis Transplant: Dr. Weilie Hu and surgeons at Guangzhou General Hospital in China performed a penis transplant on a 44-year-old man whose penis had been damaged in a traumatic accident. The donor was a 22-year-old man. Ten days after the surgery, the man had been able to urinate normally. However, the penis was removed two weeks later due to "a_severe_psychological_problem_of_the_recipient_and_his_wife." There had been no signs of rejection.*

As I nearing the end of reading the time line, he pointed then said. "This should of interest to your situation! You maybe will have real arms of your own!"

2008: First Double Arm Transplant: Between July 25 and 26, doctors at Germany's Munich University Clinic spent 15 hours grafting a pair of arms onto a 54-year-old farmer who had lost his arms just below the shoulder in the accident six years ago.

Other & Unusual Transplant Timeline Pasted from http://www.medhunters.com/articles/transplantTimelineOtherUnusual.html

That was interesting; I was thinking to myself, lately, I been wishing I had real arms. At my age I am losing my abilities to be independent, my body is not as flexible, my legs seem to be giving out lately, my vision is failing me and specially my teeth not what they used to be, they almost worn down to the gum line. It is not that they are rotten nor did not care of them, it is because I used my teeth like my hands. I unlock my pad lock with my mouth, shrew and unscrew with a shrew driver in my mouth and pretty much do a lot with my mouth. Oh well back to the argument.

He asked my interpreter to read the quotes a highlighted article that was on his desk.

She started. "XENOTRANSPLANTATION—AS A SCIENTIFIC AND ETHICAL PROBLEM **By Valery Shumakov.**

Modern methods of transplantation helped physicians to prolong the lives of about 250,000 people who had suffered from serious illnesses.

At the same time new, a rather complicated moral and ethical problem has emerged. Nowadays the most pointed problem of allografting (grafting of human organs and tissues) is that of the shortage of donor material. This is the main reason for resorting to kidney, liver or heart transplants only in cases where all resources of ordinary treatment with medical supplies or surgical operation are exhausted, and a patient is doomed to die in the near future.

"The Russian law and the supplements to it are in this sense one of the most advanced and allow to develop theory and practice of tissue transplantations keeping parity of the

donor's and recipient's interests. All should be interpreted through public consciousness. Then why today are some public figures, making use of the problem's urgency, so willing to gain political image, saying that our state is not a lawful one precisely due to the fact that in its law there is in it a presumption of consent to harvest donor tissues?"

Pasted from <http://www.ncca-kaliningrad.ru/biomediale/?blang=eng&author=shumakov>

"Is this reason for nurse Lendroma's child being here, to save her daughters" He said it so straight to me.

It finally came to me, now I understood what her words meant. "The work they do here can save my daughter, please don't kill her!" I quoted her to him.

"Yes! Her son is, so far, the only matching kidney transplant donor because of her daughter has a rare blood type. She already lost her son to sever brain damaged from a car accident; she now wants to save her daughter with his kidney." He said as he rationalized her decision.

"By helping kill her own, son!" I interjected forcibly.

"You Americans always want it both ways, you want organs or tissues at any cost, but you do not want to know where it came or how you got.

Only the rich in the western world can afford to buy life back!

She only wants the one thing left in her life, her daughter!" He said without remorse.

I was thinking of the other patients at this hospital as I said. "But, is not illegal to harvest organs or tissues of live people or dead ones, for that fact, without consent of the parents or guardians in any country?" I asked him because I was hazy in my recall of the facts.

"Mr. PR man, you are not aware that body parts harvest organs or tissues of live people for hundreds of years, even today.

We have created an official state here; this hospital is official state all by itself. The patients here are the ward of this state and thereby we are giving consent to the harvesting the tissues and organs to save lives improve the quality of lives of others, who can benefit from harvesting the tissues and organs of these children in this hospital." He professed.

"So you're selling these organs or tissues on the black market? I pressed him for an answer.

"No! Mr. PR man, we are restricted by Law, The Russian Federation Law "On Right of Children". He countered to as an answer.

Then he also retorted with an Quote, "An American of yours", citing "Nancy Scheper-Hughes, a professor of anthropology at the University of California, Berkeley, has written extensively on the human organ trade."

In his authoritative manner he continued, "In an article "The Global Traffic in Human Organs", *'Human organ trade' she writes:*

'In general, the flow of organs follows the modern routes of capital: from South to North, from Third to First World, from poor to rich, from black and brown to white and from female to male.'"

He seemed that he quoted her from memory.

Again he quotes her.

> *"In another article, "The New Cannibalism," she writes: "Indeed, there is nothing stable or sacrosanct about the 'commodity candidacy' of things. And nowhere is this more dramatically illustrated than in the booming market in human organs from both living and dead donors."*

Then he added referring to the early article:

> *". . . XENOTRANSPLANTATION, AS A SCIENTIFIC AND ETHICAL PROBLEM. "From time to time the Russian mass media publish features about the illegal home and international sale of organs and even about murders committed in the process of acquiring certain organs. It should be mentioned that none of these reports has been ever confirmed by the law-enforcement authorities."*

From his own word he pointed out the safe guards taken. "We use only military planes and soldiers under guard to transport the tissues and organs, are given to transplantation surgeon only."

He read again.

> *"Statistics prove that in economically developed countries about 150,000 people need donor organs and tissue for transplanting, while the universal need for donor material exceeds these figures many times.*

About 30,000 people in the USA and about 6,000 in the UK are put on a waiting list in expectation of donor heart, kidneys, lungs or liver, but only 10% of them stand a better chance by waiting until the transplant happens. According to, Doctor Valery Shumakov, one of our own, well-known Surgeon, he also won the international gold medal Outstanding World Surgeon. He was the founding father of organ transplants in Russia." He stopped and proudly added. "He is my mentor"

"This as doubled since 1988, it keeps on increasing, adding 15% to the total rate annually, while the claim is met only in 5-6% of cases even in the group of patients younger than 65." All the facts and numbers rolled again from his learned brain.

"May I read this, from his paper . . . ?" He fishes a plastic sleeve containing quotes for his presentations, from his desk. He Skips down from the one already told me

". . . XENOTRANSPLANTATION, AS A SCIENTIFIC AND ETHICAL PROBLEM. Another problem lies in the high price for donor material and the operation itself. In the USA kidney transplants cost about 90,000 dollars, to say nothing of the expenses afterwards—7,000 dollars makes up the annual payment for the medication necessary to prevent organ rejection, and which a patient requires for the rest of his life. In Russia the cost of a kidney transplant today is no less than 250,000 roubles, and payment for expensive imported remedies is to be added to the sum. That is why kidney transplants in this country are mainly sponsored by the health authorities, though as a rule they are short of financial resources as well. For this reason the number of such operations has notably reduced here. Famine prices made organ transplants inaccessible to the ordinary person, who works on a limited budget, even if he is doomed to die without the operation." Pasted from <http://www.ncca-kaliningrad.ru/biomediale/?blang=eng&author=shumakov>

"Look at this book, this is only one of over of 12 such books showing what each child here has done in providing their organs so the lives of other." He said like a proud papa showing family photos.

He pushed a large 4-5 inch binder and turned it around for me, then slowly turned the pages of plastic protectors of the photos and letters, which I could not read, but my interpreter quickly read bits and pieces of letters from children and adults who received transplants from the children here.

"We are not comfortable on what we have to do here, but we know, because of our work, thousands of people and especially children have happier and live healthier lives because of the sacrifices these children made in losing their lives." He beseeched me.

There were many before and after pictures, you could not help to think what would to them if they did not receive a transplant.

"For this reason, this why we exist, 'They Live to Die, to Save Another!" He Proclaimed then added one more quote, *"Life and death enjoy equal rights, they cannot get along without each other",—N.I. Pirogov (1835),""Death serves the prolongation of the human being's life" (Pokrovsky V., 1997)*.

What about Blinker?

"What about Blinker?" I said, "You guys fuck up! He was not a vegetable, he could communicate!", my heart was burning in hatred of his system.

"That was a failure on our part," we should have been more through in our testing, I will take the blame!" he said in a way that he felt the pain of the lost of Blinker as we did.

The three of us felt resigned, as we all knew there was nothing more to do about Blinker.

CHAPTER 23

The Conclusion

I do not know where I stand on issue of transplantology, I am sure, one-way or another, the same thing is happening all-over the world, even the U.S., we just do not know about it.

You only have to ask yourself: "What would I really do to save someone you love dearly or your own life, if one who life and health depended on life of another child who seem to have no life at all!

Enough money can buy life of another, even if they are murdered! Can harvesting body parts from animals or vegetated person help cut the death toll to otherwise healthy people to save those in need of a organ to live a better life?

I just know every time I see a child with blue eyes and she or he winks at me. I think are they the blue eyes of Blinker?

ABOUT THE AUTHOR

The author bring an unique experiences in his book, "Blue Eyes", having lost his both arms as a child, as he grew up in and out of the disabled care systems.

Out of the dependence of the system, the author brings over 43 years of experience working with the disabled in designing, founding, directing and consulting recreational programs as well as counseling.

The author draws much from his own personal experiences, adding a new disabled prospective to the world of his fiction characters as he explore the many subject he had experienced firsthand, the world of the Disabled, Nudism (folklore and history of nudism, especially of that of Russia), Disabled Sexuality, life experiences and the including varied of personalities he had in his disabled world.

Author, now engaged to **Thongbai (May) Boontem**, native of Si Sa Ket, Thailand.

MATERIALS AND REFERENCES
USED IN THIS BOOK

The majority of these quoted materials and references are used without permission of their authors. Every effort was made to get permission of the author as outline by the "Fair Use Act". Some have not or others don't care replied to my e-mails. Some materials were given or sent to me via e-mail. So, if I use a quote I referenced as best as I could the material or quotes as being theirs. All material or quotes used or plagiarized are in italic in the text of this book.

My apologies in advance if, your unhappy with the use of your materials or quotes without your permission. If I need to, I will re-write your material or quotes upon your request. Please contact me as soon as possible at my addresses below if there is a problem.

I thank those authors in advance for allowing articles and to be using your materials or quotes without direct permission.

—Frederick H. Gilbert, author of "Blue Eyes".

Frederick Gilbert
384/61 Laguna Homes
T. San-Sai, A. San—Noi
Chiang Mai, Thailand 50210
My Cell Phone: 011 + 0823849843
My E-mail: capthooksthai@yahoo.com

Page No.   Materials and references used:

54   "The staffs in these institutions are called "cleaners," and it is clear that children are being cared for, but only in the sense of custodial care." A direct quote used without permission of the author in his paper ""Imperfect' children left to die" by Mark Franchetti, Moscow, The Center for Defense Information (CDI) is a division of the World Security Institute
Pasted from <http://www.cdi.org/russia/johnson/3061.html>

67   5 Selected paragraphs or excerpts from Violence and Children with Disabilities:—An International Perspective A direct quote used without permission of the author.
Pasted from <http://www.riglobal.org/publications2/10_24. htm>

68   Quote cited from MDIR Publication "Observations"
Pasted from <http://www.mdri.org/mdri-web-2007/ publications/Russia3.html>

The following selected direct quotes and paraphrasing were used without permission of the author.

90-   Four articles by Paul Jenson, San Diego, California, 1998
1. Introduction **Pasted from <http://www.russiannudist naturist.com/introduction.htm>**
2. Wedding **Pasted from <http://www.russiannudist naturist.com/wedding.htm>**
3. The Eve of Ivana-Kupala **Pasted from <http://www. russiannudistnaturist.com/eveofivanakupala.htm>**
4. Interview: M. Rusinov **Pasted from <http://www.russian nudistnaturist.com/interviewrusinov.htm>**

Passages were use or plagiarized from selected direct quotes used without permission of the author.

95-   Two quotes used from "Beautiful Russian nudists" Added: "Search Your Love"11/06/2006,
Pasted from <http://www.syl.com/articles/beautifulrussian nudists.html>

| 117 | Passages were use or plagiarized from selected direct quotes used without permission of the author. |
| 101 | Paraphrased: "They have no mothers or fathers to kiss them good night: their parents abandoned them rather than face the stigma of bringing up an "imperfect" child in a society that abhorred disability in Soviet times and is little different today. **The Sunday Times (UK), 'Imperfect' children left to die" by Mark Franchetti Moscow February 21 1999,** |

Passages were use from selected direct quotes used without permission of the author.

103-107	Other & Unusual Transplant Timeline **Pasted from http://www.medhunters.com/articles/transplantTimeline OtherUnusual.html**
107	"Xenotransplantation—As A Scientific And Ethical Problem", By Valery Shumakov. "Biomediale. Contemporary Society and Genomic Culture". Edited and curated by Dmitry Bulatov. The National Centre for Contemporary art (Kaliningrad branch, Russia), The National Publishing House "Yantarny Skaz": Kaliningrad, 2004. ISBN 5-7406-0853-7 **Pasted from <http://www.ncca-kaliningrad.ru/biomediale/?blang=eng&author=shumakov**
109	'The Global Traffic in Human Organs' Nancy Scheper-Hughes, a professor of anthropology at the University of California, Berkeley, quoted from an article "Human organs: the next futures market? By Joanne Laurier, 26 April 2002, appearing in World Socialist Web Site. Copyright 1998-2008 by World Socialist Web Site All rights reserved [Wrote, but no reply] **Pasted from <http://www.wsws.org/articles/2002/apr2002/body-a26.shtml>**
110-111	Three quotes from "Xenotransplantation—As A Scientific And Ethical Problem" By Valery Shumakov. "Biomediale.
118	Contemporary Society and Genomic Culture". Edited and curated by Dmitry Bulatov. The National Centre for Contemporary art (Kaliningrad branch, Russia), The National Publishing House "Yantarny Skaz": Kaliningrad, 2004. ISBN

5-7406-0853-7 **Pasted from <http://www.ncca-kaliningrad. ru/biomediale/?blang=eng&author=shumakov**

111   Use title of his article "Death serves the prolongation of the human being's life" (Pokrovsky V., 1997). Quoted from an article "Legal Aspects Of Tissue Transplantation" Nigmatullin R.T., Chernov N.V., State Institution—Russian Eye and Plastic Surgery Centre of the Russian Public Health Ministry, Ufa-city.

111   "Life and death enjoy equal rights, they can not get along without each other." A quote from "Legal Aspects Of Tissue Transplantation", Nigmatullin R.T., Chernov N.V., State Institution—Russian Eye and Plastic Surgery Centre of the Russian Public Health Ministry, Ufa-city.